FIFTY
MYSTERIES

||||||||||||||||||||||||||||||||||||||||

THE ANGELA FILES

DOGWOOD
PRESS

Also by John M. Floyd

Deception
Clockwork
Midnight
Rainbow's End

FIFTY
MYSTERIES

|||||||||||||||||||||||||||||||||||||||||||||||||||||||||||||

THE ANGELA FILES

John M. Floyd

DOGWOOD PRESS

Library of Congress Control Number
2014942037

Printed in the United States of America

Cover design by Joe Lee and Cyndi Clark
Cover photo © iStockphoto/DNY59

First Dogwood Press edition October 2014

DOGWOOD
PRESS

DOGWOOD PRESS
P.O. Box 5958 • Brandon, MS 39047
www.dogwoodpress.com

For Gabriel and Richard

ACKNOWLEDGMENTS

I owe special thanks to a number of people for this book. First is my publisher, Joe Lee, who several years ago came up with the idea of eventually collecting some of my Angela Potts/Chunky Jones mysteries together into a single volume; another is my e-friend Dan Persinger, who recently not only suggested such a collection but also recommended that it be done in a unique and interactive format, with the mysteries first and the solutions in a separate section; yet another is Johnene Granger, the fiction editor of *Woman's World*, who had the (in my opinion, anyway) good judgment to publish so many installments of this series in her magazine. Mostly, though, I sincerely thank the many kind fans at conferences and signings who have expressed an interest in seeing an entire book featuring Ms. Potts and Sheriff Jones. It was you folks who made this happen.

I am also indebted, as always, to my wife Carolyn for her support and her proofreading. If not for either of those two things, my fiction manuscripts would probably still be sitting unpublished in my home office or our bedroom closet, aging like tobacco leaves.

The following stories in this book first appeared (three of them under different titles) in *Woman's World*, 2011-2014: "Wild Goose Chase," "Caught on Tape," "Gone Goes the Weasel," "Stick 'Em Up," "A Shot in the Dark," "Par for the Course," "A Quick Stop," "In Other Words," "A Dirty Trick," "Angela's Taxi," "The Cover-Up," "The Truth Stings," "Turn Right at the Light," "Watch Your Step," "The Family Jewels," "The Listener," "Picture This," "As Clear as Mud," "An Inside Job," "License to Steal," "Checkmate," "Going for the Gold," and "Hildy's Fortune." The rest of them are new, and have never before been published.

INTRODUCTION

Thirteen years ago the weekly magazine *Woman's World* published the following words, the first two paragraphs of the first installment of a series I wrote for them:

Angela Potts was always the first to see trouble coming.

A retired schoolteacher, she pictured herself as a lone sailor stationed on the bow, watching for rocks and icebergs in the fog. In reality, her lookout point was the wooden swing on her front porch. From there she monitored the usually calm seas of her hometown, alert for any sign of a threat.

That story appeared in their September 18, 2001, issue (exactly a week after our world changed forever), and since then Angela and a guy she had taught in the fifth grade—a kid who had grown up to become the sheriff of their small southern town—have teamed up to solve dozens of mysteries. My/their unnamed little town might look calm, but it's turned out to have a lot of secrets and a lot of lawbreakers.

Angela is an unlikely sleuth but an interesting lady: retired, demanding, mischievous, energetic, and cunning. Her former student, Sheriff Charles "Chunky" Jones, is none of those things—but he's basically okay as long as he has somebody to prod him along a bit. The fact that their adventures have become popular with so many readers (and believe me, I'm grateful, to them and to Lady Luck as well) has led directly to this book: a collection of fifty Angela/Chunky mystery cases that I hope will challenge you as much as they challenged our hero and heroine.

More than anything, though, my wish is that you will enjoy reading these stories as much as I enjoyed writing them.

John M. Floyd
March 2014

CONTENTS

1

WILD GOOSE CHASE

SHERIFF Charles Jones was reading the comics in the newspaper when part-time amateur sleuth and full-time pain-in-the-rear-end Angela Potts—Angel, to her friends—pushed through the door of his office. He looked up and frowned. "What do *you* want?"

She stared at him. "That's a fine greeting, to a citizen, a taxpayer, and your former teacher."

"Sorry." He lowered his paper and gave her a sweet smile. "What do *you* want?"

"I want a slice of German chocolate cake. But I'll settle"—she dug around in her purse and pulled out a coin jar—"for a donation to the Women's League."

The sheriff went back to his frown and his newspaper.

"Sorry. I gave already at the office."

"This *is* your office," she said.

The ringing phone saved him. He answered it—and froze. He sat there, eyes wide, listening. Finally he said, "Thanks, Jimbo," and hung up.

"Who was that?" Angela asked.

He put his paper aside and ran a hand through his hair. "Jimmy Boteler—he runs the gas station out on the highway, near the prison. He said one of his customers' cars was stolen a few minutes ago."

"What?"

"He said a teenaged girl was sitting in the line waiting for a gas pump when Goose Garvey—remember him?—ran up and pulled her out of her Jeep and threw her to the ground and drove off down the road."

"But Garvey's locked up," she said. "He's doing five years for mail fraud."

"Not at the moment. He broke out. Right now old Goose is flying south, in a red Jeep Wrangler."

"Is the girl okay?"

"Yeah, just hoppin' mad." The sheriff reached for the desk phone. "I gotta call the state cops."

"You also gotta chase this guy. That gas station's only five minutes away."

"How? One of my deputies is in Jackson at a seminar, the other's at Auto Zone replacing his headlight. And my car's in the shop."

Angela rolled her eyes. "The Three Stooges," she said. "Come on, we'll take mine."

Seven minutes later, in Angela's ancient Buick, they blew past Jimmy Boteler's Texaco, headed south. Thinking aloud, she said, "Goose grew up here—he must know there's nothing but cottonfields and swampland for the next forty miles."

"So?"

"So we'll catch him," she said.

The sheriff stared at her from the passenger seat. "You think we'll catch him, in this—no offense—piece of junk?"

"Yep," she said, her eyes on the road. "Because we'll outsmart him."

"We?"

"*I'll* outsmart him," she corrected.

He just shook his head. "No way."

"Way," she said. "He made a mistake—and now I know what he has to do."

"You want to share that with the rest of the class?"

She grinned. "How about a bet? If you're right, I buy you a loaded pizza. If I'm right, and we catch him, you buy me lunch at Roscoe's. This is gumbo day."

"We already had lunch," he said.

"I could eat again. I'm a growing girl."

"I sure hope not," he murmured.

"What did you say!?"

"I said I sure hope the pizza's hot."

Ten miles farther, in the middle of nowhere, she swerved into the crowded parking lot of a diner—the first sign of life they'd seen since passing the gas station. "There he is," she said, pointing.

The sheriff gasped. Sure enough, a red Jeep was sitting right there in the lot; its driver was watching the restaurant. At that moment, an elderly lady emerged with a milkshake in her hand and beeped open the door of a parked Ford. The Jeep's door opened as well, and as Goose Garvey climbed out in his orange prison coveralls and approached the lady, Angela screeched her car up beside him. Sheriff Jones hopped out and drew his pistol, and a minute later Garvey was handcuffed and fuming in the back seat of Angela's Buick.

Afterward, the sheriff turned to Angela. "It's answer time. How'd you know he would stop?"

"You owe me lunch," she said. "I'll tell you at Roscoe's."

MYSTERY:
||||||||||||||||||||||||||||||||||||||

Why was Angela so sure they would catch the escapee?

2

CAUGHT ON TAPE

Detective Daniel Bradshaw of the state police was pouring himself a cup of coffee in the sheriff's office when Sheriff Jones stomped in. "Make yourself at home, Lieutenant," the sheriff said.

Bradshaw took a sip and grimaced. "I've served prisoners better coffee than this." He slouched into a chair. "Where you been?"

"Over at the hospital, interviewing Ms. Langley. She told me you'd already questioned her."

Bradshaw shrugged. "I was in town anyway, and heard about the incident."

Sixty-year-old Miriam Langley had been attacked from behind in her driveway last night, and her purse stolen. As she struggled, and before she was knocked unconscious—struck above the left ear—she said she looked down and glimpsed a pair of mud-streaked sneakers just like the ones worn by her teenaged neighbor, Billy Moore.

"Moore's our man," Bradshaw added. "I've sent your deputy to bring him in."

"*You* sent *my* deputy?"

"I figured you wouldn't mind if—"

"Well, well. Danny Bradshaw," a voice said. "Something odd this way comes."

Both men turned to see Angela Potts standing in the doorway. Bradshaw's face hardened. "The crimefighter herself," he said.

"I am but a poor peasant," Angela said sweetly. "You still upset about the Joe Fairley case?"

"You interfered with a murder investigation, Ms. Potts."

"And solved it," she reminded him. "Along with Chunky, that is."

Bradshaw frowned. "Chunky?"

"Along with Sheriff Jones," Angela corrected.

The sheriff gave her a dark look, then cleared his throat and said, "Ms. Potts knows the victim, Lieutenant. She's spoken with her, at my request."

"I also know her neighbor," Angela said. "And he's no mugger."

Bradshaw smirked. "You're saying Billy Moore's innocent?"

"That's right."

"Even though Ms. Langley identified him?"

"She didn't *see* him. She saw someone wearing the same brand of shoes."

Bradshaw looked bored. "You have any evidence at all that would suggest Moore isn't guilty?"

Angela took a videocassette from her purse and handed it to the sheriff. "I got this from Bert Fitzhugh, manager of the pizza place on East Hamilton. It's a surveillance tape, from last night—I just finished watching it. Billy Moore often goes there, and I wanted to check something."

"*You* wanted to? Who runs this office, Sheriff, you or your old schoolteacher?"

"By 'old,'" Angela said, eyes squinted, "I hope you meant 'former.'"

Sheriff Jones could feel a headache coming on. Dutifully, he plugged the cassette into a TV/VCR combination unit. A view appeared onscreen of a fast-food counter and two cash registers.

"Fitz installed the camera last year," Angela explained, "to catch an employee he suspected of embezzlement."

Bradshaw snorted. "What good is this? You want to see if they shortchanged any customers last night?"

"Run it forward a bit," Angela told the sheriff. "And watch the mirror."

He immediately saw what she meant: reflected in a long mirrored wall beside the registers were several diners seated at tables, chowing down. "That's Billy Moore," she said, pointing. "And look at his shoes."

Both men leaned forward, peering at the tape. "No mud there that I can see," the sheriff said.

"Right. Miriam said the sneakers she saw were muddy. And this was taped"—she pointed to the timestamp on the screen—"an hour after her assault."

"You gotta be kidding me." Detective Bradshaw looked at Angela. "You think this proves anything? He probably cleaned his shoes off before he came in."

Angela started to reply, but Bradshaw said, "And another thing. Since the victim was hit from behind, the injury above the left ear implies her attacker was left-handed. Correct?" This time *he* was the one pointing to the actions on the screen. "This shows Moore holding his pizza with his left hand. His drinking cup too." Bradshaw sat back and sipped his coffee, grinning. "You're not so smart after all, Ms. Potts. This tape will help convict him."

Angela stared back at him. "Thirty-five years ago, Danny, I taught your mother, in the schoolhouse two blocks from here. I wish you were a tenth as smart as she was."

"What do you mean?"

"I've just shown you proof," she said, "that Billy Moore is innocent."

MYSTERY:
||||||||||||||||||||||||||||||||

What proof was Angela referring to?

3

IT'S ABOUT TIME

Sheriff Charles Jones climbed out of his cruiser just as Angela Potts steered her huge car into the parking space beside him. He tried to ignore her, but she hopped out and said, "What are *you* doing here?"

It was a good question: they were standing in front of the Shady Orchard Retirement Home.

"Police business," he said, staring at her twenty-year-old, eighteen-foot-long Buick. "Tell me, do Navy pilots ever try to land on this thing by mistake?"

"Don't change the subject. What kind of police business?"

He frowned. "Did you follow me here?"

"I wish." She rolled her eyes. "I'm here for my cousin

Gladys's birthday party."

"You sound thrilled."

"Can I borrow your gun? I might have to shoot my way out."

"Sorry, you're on your own." He started to turn away.

Angela stamped her foot. "Come on, Chunky, tell me why you're here."

"No. And don't call me Chunky."

"Why not? It's your name."

"It was a *nick*name. Long ago. And why I'm here is none of your—"

"Tell me," she said solemnly, "and you will find inner peace."

He sighed and rubbed his eyes. "All *right*. I'm going to see Bernie Walton. Remember him?"

"Sure. His wife Earline and I taught school together."

"I know. You both taught *me*." He paused, thinking. "You seen her lately?"

"Earline?" Angela snorted. "She flies by on her broom now and then."

Sheriff Jones nodded. "I know what you mean—old Bernie's probably lucky they divorced."

"They're still friends, though. I'm not sure for how long."

"What?"

"Word is, Earline's thinking about changing her will," Angela said. "Maybe cutting out her daughter."

"Who is also Bernie's daughter."

"Yep." She studied him. "What's all this about, Chunky?"

He hesitated, then said, "Bernie Walton found Earline's body at eight this morning, after he walked to her house for breakfast."

Angela gasped. "You're kidding."

"She'd been stabbed. Coroner says time of death was sometime last night, probably around ten."

"Could Bernie be a suspect? Because of the will?"

The sheriff frowned, considering that. "I don't really think so. He seemed pretty upset, earlier." He patted the pocket that held his notepad. "I only have a couple questions for him."

At that moment Bernie shuffled out of the building, spotted them, and said, "Hi, Sheriff. I been expecting you." He made his shaky way to one of the two benches near the entrance, sagged onto it, and nodded to Angela. "Hello, Angel. Guess you two must've heard what happened."

Angela and the sheriff walked over and sat facing him, several feet away. Bernie was wearing the blue windbreaker and black baseball cap that he seemed to wear everywhere, and both hands were propped on the crooked end of a walking stick.

"I'm sorry for your loss, Bernie," she said.

"Me too." He sat motionless a moment, then focused on the sheriff. "What is it you need to know?"

Sheriff Jones produced a notepad and pen. "For one thing, when did you last see your wife?"

"Alive, you mean?"

"Yes."

"Last night," Bernie said.

The sheriff frowned. "Last night?"

"We walked down to the café for a piece of pie around nine, and I left her at her house not long after. Then I came back here and went to bed."

He jotted this into his notebook and asked, "What was her frame of mind, when you left her? Worried?

Scared? Depressed?"

"She seemed fine."

"Bernie," Angela said, with eyes narrowed, "what's that on your jacket?"

He followed her gaze. Just below the left pocket of his windbreaker was a reddish smear. He blinked in obvious surprise, then said sadly, "I knelt beside her body when I found her. I guess I must've brushed against her, and . . ." He swallowed and looked as if he might be about to cry.

The sheriff closed his notepad. "That's enough for now, Mr. Walton. Much obliged."

He and Angela stood and watched the old man rise from his bench and hobble into the building.

"I feel sorry for him," the sheriff said.

"Me too. But I'd search his room, if I were you."

"For what?"

"The murder weapon," she said. "I think he's the one who killed her."

MYSTERY
||||||||||||||||||||||||||||||

Why did Angela suspect Bernie Walton?

4

GONE GOES THE WEASEL

Retired teacher and amateur investigator Angela Potts arrived in Sheriff Jones's office to find him leaned back in his chair and scowling. Without changing expression he looked at her and said, "As if I don't have enough problems."

"Well, thanks a lot."

"I didn't mean you." He held up a sheet of paper from his desktop. "Last night somebody stole the weasel off its pedestal in the high school gym."

"The what?"

"You know, the team mascot. The big stuffed weasel."

"It's an otter, Chunky. The team's called the Otters."

He snorted. "Not when I played ball there. We were

the Tigers—what's wrong with that name? Besides, it looks like a weasel to me."

"I seem to remember you were the team's water boy."

His face reddened. "I was still on the roster." He handed her the piece of paper. "Here—this was left at the scene."

Printed on the sheet were the words FOR SHERIFF JONES, followed by a poem:

> I'm Mexico bound,
> But if I'm to be found,
> Just whittle me down
> And then turn me around.

It was signed NORA MICHAEL.

"Who's Nora Michael?" Angela said.

"Don't ask me. A phony name, probably—but why sign it at all? And why write a poem like that? What does it mean?—Find her, stab her, and bring her back home?"

"Could be a clue," she said.

"I might agree, if there was any fingerprints on the note—"

"If there *were* any fingerprints on the note," she corrected.

"But there wasn't."

"*Weren't*," she said.

He added, "What could a stuffed animal like that be worth, anyway? Where could you sell it?"

"This wasn't about money." Angela returned the note to his desk. "Looks like somebody arrogant is trying to embarrass the school—or *you*."

"Somebody rebelling against authority, you mean."

"Or just wanting attention."

"Sounds pretty foolhardy, to me," he said.

Angela shrugged. "It's a riddle."

"A what?"

"Whoever did it is saying *solve this, if you can.*" She looked at him and said, "The thief's taunting you. Daring you to catch her—or him."

The sheriff sighed and rubbed his eyes. "I really, really don't need this."

"What you need," she said, "is to put a stop to these pranks. They waste everybody's time."

"Prank or not, it's still a robbery. The principal's mad as a hornet." He held up another sheet of paper. "You know Teresa Garver?"

"She's new. An English teacher."

"Well, she hosted a student committee meeting in the gymnasium last night to plan the Junior-Senior banquet. She had to leave the meeting early, but she gave me a list of the attendees."

"And?"

"They were the only people to use the gym last night," he said. "Ms. Garver said the weasel—"

"Otter."

"—was in its assigned place when she left around eight o'clock, but the cleaning crew says when they arrived an hour later, it was gone."

"How about security cameras?" Angela asked.

"There are plenty of them in the classroom buildings—but none in the gym or parking lot."

The list he handed to her contained seven names: Jo Nell Gorman, Kevin Higa, Stuart King, Brittany Rae Bourgeois, Joseph Cook, Leah Jean Cimaron, and Allison Wingo.

Angela was quiet a moment, studying the sheet and frowning. "I know most of these kids. Kevin and Stu have been in some trouble, but nothing serious. The Cook boy's kind of weird, and so's Leah. I think Allie Wingo's the senior class president—"

"Since I doubt that part about Mexico, I figure the suspect's still right here in school," the sheriff said. "Ms. Garver volunteered to help me talk to all seven of them, and to their parents."

Angela had a sudden thought—and smiled. "I don't think you'll have to."

"Why?"

"Because we aren't quite as dumb as one of these students thinks we are."

"What do you mean?"

She handed him the list. "I know," she said, "who stole the mascot."

MYSTERY:

Who was the thief?

5

STICK 'EM UP

AT 9:30 a.m. retired schoolteacher Angela Potts entered Roscoe's Cafe and plopped down at a table across from Sheriff Charles Jones. Banjo music blared from a radio behind the counter.

"Late breakfast?" she asked, watching the sheriff shovel down pancakes.

"Brunch."

Angela winced at the jangling music. "Roscoe," she shouted, "is it true that you were one of the extras in *Deliverance?*"

A voice called, from somewhere in the kitchen: "The sheriff got my part—I was working that day."

Sheriff Jones kept chewing. "I wasn't even born yet.

You two think you're funny, don't you?"

Before she could reply, his cell phone buzzed. He answered the call, listened a moment, and gasped. "I'm on my way," he blurted.

"Chunky?" Angela said. "What's wrong?"

"Don't call me Chunky," he said. He stood, pocketed his phone, and hitched his belt a little higher.

"What's the matter?"

"The bank's been robbed."

First National was only a block away. They arrived to find the manager, a security guard, and two tellers standing in a nervous group. Around 9:15, they said, a man wearing a baseball cap and sunglasses had come in carrying a briefcase in each hand. He'd walked straight to Judy Harrison—the younger teller—and demanded she fill both cases with large bills. Minutes later he'd hurried out with a small fortune.

"Did he show a weapon?" the sheriff asked.

"No, he never let go of the briefcases," Judy said, near tears. "Even while I was filling them. But he told me he had a gun."

He glanced around. "Security cameras?"

"No," the manager said.

"And where were you?" the sheriff asked the guard—his nametag said J. BRADLEY.

Bradley's face reddened. "On my break. I'd gone out back for a smoke."

"Do you break the same time every day?" Angela asked him.

"No—it was just bad luck."

"Maybe." To the others she said, "How long after the guard left did this happen? Anyone remember?"

"I do," said Ethel Williams, the older teller. "Mr.

Bradley was barely out the back door when the robber came in the front."

"That makes sense. Somebody probably tipped him off." Angela turned to Deputy Fred Prewitt, who had just arrived, and said, "Fred, find out from the phone company if there were any outgoing calls from the bank lobby around nine-fifteen."

Meanwhile, the sheriff asked Judy for a description of the suspect. She frowned, thinking. "Early thirties, I guess. Stocky, green eyes, dark hair. And a blue jacket."

"Judy's more observant than I am," Ethel said, "but I also saw khaki pants. And boots."

"Anybody see his vehicle, afterward?" the sheriff asked. No one had. He was mulling things over when Deputy Prewitt returned, notepad in hand.

"Two calls went out, at nine-ten and nine-fourteen," he reported. "The first was to a number on Magnolia Street, from the branch manager's office—"

"That's my house," the manager agreed. "I called my wife."

"—and the other was to a mobile number, from . . ." Prewitt walked behind the counter and checked the numbers on the two phones. "This teller station."

"That's mine," Ethel said, and gulped when she realized what that meant. Everyone turned to look at her.

"But I wasn't even *at* my station," she said. "I was checking the ATM just before the guy came in."

"You're saying someone else could've used your phone?" Angela asked.

"I'm just saying *I* didn't," Ethel said.

"Well, it won't matter. If we have the robber's cell number, and his phone's still on, maybe we can try to pinpoint his location. Right, Fred?"

Prewitt nodded. "We sure can."

"We'll catch him and *ask* him who his accomplice was."

At that, Judy's face turned a whiter shade of pale.

Angela stared at her and said quietly, "Or would you rather confess now?"

Judy's eyes widened. "What? I didn't—"

"Read her her rights, Chunky."

When Deputy Prewitt had led the stunned teller away, both the branch manager and the sheriff turned to Angela. "How'd you know?" they asked, in unison.

Angela smiled. "Judy might be observant," she said, "but she's not very bright."

MYSTERY:
||||||||||||||||||||||||||||||||||||

Why did Angela suspect that Judy was the accomplice?

HIGH FINANCE

ANGELA Potts liked Los Angeles. Not enough to live there—she liked small towns a lot better—but she enjoyed visiting her older sister Helen once every few years. At the moment Angela was seated in her nephew Willy's office in downtown L.A., waiting for Helen to arrive. Willy, who had picked her up at the airport an hour ago, was a pleasant but high-strung young man with a management position at a brokerage firm. And he was dressed for the part.

Angela, studying his tie and three-piece suit, asked, "You going to a funeral?"

Willy looked up from his computer. "We all look this way. Our firm's ultra-conservative."

"They allow galoshes, I hope." She pointed her furled umbrella at his wet tenth-floor window. "I thought it never rained in Southern California."

"Well, I thought everybody was friendly in the South, too, until I got my laptop stolen in Birmingham last year."

"Must've been a tourist," she said. She glanced up at the wall clock. 4:45. The three of them planned to have dinner together, then drive out to Helen's house in the San Fernando Valley.

Willy was pecking away on his keyboard when his phone rang. He picked it up, listened, then sat up straight. "I'll be right there." He hung up and said, "Stay here, Aunt Angela."

"What's the matter, Willy?"

He was already halfway to the door. "Some stock certificates are missing, and one of our managers reported seeing someone strange in the hall. Security guard thinks the thief might still be on this floor." He paused and gave her a pained look. "And call me William, okay?"

"I'll come with—"

"No," he said. "Stay, and lock the door. I'll be back."

Moments later, standing in the office doorway, Angela saw a red-faced man in a sport coat and jeans sprinting toward her. Immediately she stepped into the hallway and blocked his path.

He lurched to a breathless stop. "Excuse me, please."

"What's your name?" she asked.

He raised his chin. "Reynolds Whitworth. Who are you?"

"I'm the boss's aunt," she lied. "What's the hurry?"

He hesitated, then snapped, "A client from New York wants to buy ten thousand shares of a tech stock *right now*, that's the hurry. And the exchange closes in ten minutes. May I pass, please?"

Angela stepped aside, but as the flustered man started to dash past her she reached down and snagged his sneakered foot with the crook of her umbrella. He tripped, blurted an extremely rude word, and whacked his forehead soundly against the steel rim of a water fountain five feet away.

She knelt beside the sprawled, now-unconscious man and rolled him face-up. "Willy!" she shouted, over her shoulder.

Seconds later her nephew appeared, goggle-eyed and open-mouthed. "What happened? Who's that?"

Angela stood and adjusted her hat. "You know anybody named Reynolds Whitworth?"

"No. Should I?"

She pointed with her umbrella. "Take a look inside his pockets."

"What?"

"Are you deaf? Check his pockets."

His eyes grew even wider. "I can't do that."

She let out a weary sigh. "Are you sure you're my nephew?" She knelt again and did a quick search. From an inside coat pocket she removed a thick sheaf of folded documents. She rose and handed them to Willy. "Is this what's missing?"

He flipped through them, aghast. "*Yes!* These are the certificates." He stared down at the thief. A small crowd was forming around them. "How did this happen? Did he knock himself out?"

"I helped a little," she said.

"But—how did you *know*?"

"Well, he was running, for one thing."

"And?"

She pointed again. "He's wearing blue jeans and sneakers."

"What?"

"That doesn't look ultra-conservative to me."

Willy stared at her. "You suspected him . . . because of his blue jeans?"

"I doubted that he *worked* here because of his blue jeans. I *suspected* him because of something he told me."

"What did he tell you?"

She grinned. "Something no trader would have said."

MYSTERY:
||||||||||||||||||||||||||||||||||||

Why did Angela figure "Reynolds Whitworth"
was the guilty party?

7

A SHOT IN THE DARK

SELF-PROCLAIMED sleuth Angela Potts stared drowsily at the black forest passing by outside the patrol car's window. It was barely five a.m. "Are we still on the map?" she asked.

The driver—Sheriff Charles Jones—snorted. "Don't worry. Christopher Columbus is my middle name."

"If I recall, he didn't know where he was either."

Before the sheriff could reply, they saw lights ahead. He slowed and parked in a gravel driveway beside his deputy's cruiser. "Earlier, you asked why I brought you along," he said, and pointed. "That's it. Eleanor Willard's house."

"What's so special about Eleanor Willard?"

"She's dead," he said.

They found Deputy Fred Prewitt in the doorway of a dimly-lit bedroom. The elderly Ms. Willard sat slumped in a chair with a .22 revolver on the floor beside it. "Single gunshot wound to the head," Prewitt told them. "The serial number's been filed off." He added that he'd spotted her through an open window after responding to an anonymous call from "a neighbor who'd heard a shot." The coroner was on his way.

"Something's fishy, here," Angela said.

Prewitt nodded. "I know. First, there are no neighbors out here close enough to *hear* a gunshot. Second, why shoot yourself when there's a medicine cabinet nearby with enough drugs to kill an elephant? Third, her bedroom window was open. Fourth, the gun she used is untraceable."

Angela raised an eyebrow. "Murder?"

"Possibly," the sheriff said. "But by who?"

"By whom," she said. Then: "Have you identified the number of the tipoff call?"

"Even more fishy. Caller ID pointed us to the office phone at a motel five miles south. I called them—the desk clerk had been in the restroom. Nobody saw anybody."

Prewitt glanced out the window. "Car coming."

The new arrival was Ms. Willard's nephew George Glenn, a local businessman. Angela and Sheriff Jones met him on the front porch.

"It's your Aunt Eleanor," the sheriff told him. "I tried calling you—"

"I've been out jogging. What happened?"

"She's dead, Mr. Glenn. An apparent suicide, about two hours ago."

Glenn's eyes bugged out.

"Is she normally alone here?" Angela asked him.

Glenn swallowed, looking stunned. "Yes. Yes, I come check on her every morning."

The sheriff nodded. "Glad you did. My deputy's inside—he'll need your fingerprints."

"Fingerprints?"

"To rule out foul play."

Glenn blinked. "You think *I* shot her?"

"It's routine. To distinguish your prints from any others we might find."

"Oh." He still looked dazed but seemed to have calmed down.

"Notice any strange behavior, lately?" the sheriff asked, as Prewitt joined them. "Anger? Depression?"

Glenn shrugged. "Sometimes, I guess."

"Did she have any enemies?"

"No."

"Did she own a firearm?"

"I don't know."

"We'll know soon," Angela said. At that, everyone turned to look at her.

"What do you mean?" Glenn asked.

"Criminals often use gloves, or wipe things down afterward. But *before* the crime—well, they're usually careless."

"How?"

"We have the pistol, with the cartridges still in the cylinder," she said. "If the gun's not Ms. Willard's, we can assume it was loaded by whoever shot her. And I'd bet my late husband's pension that those shells have the killer's fingerprints on them."

Dead silence. George Glenn's face, so composed a

moment earlier, had suddenly turned gray. He swallowed and staggered backward against the porch rail.

Angela waited a moment, then said carefully, "Why'd you do it, Mr. Glenn?"

His shoulders sagged. He knew he was caught. "She was going to cut me out of her will," he murmured. "After all I've *done* for her . . ."

The two lawmen gaped at him. "Fred," the sheriff said finally, "read him his rights."

Later, alone with Angela in the patrol car, Sheriff Jones said, "You ever seen a twenty-two caliber cartridge, Ms. Potts?"

She looked at him. "Sure I have. Why?"

"They're too small for credible fingerprints to be lifted off them."

"I know that," she said. "But Glenn didn't."

"So accusing him was just a bluff? A shot in the dark?"

She smiled and raised one eyebrow. "Not exactly."

MYSTERY:
||||||||||||||||||||||||||||||||||

Why did Angela already suspect that
George Glenn was the killer?

8

PURPLE MARTIN

SHERIFF Charles Jones stopped his cruiser at the curb six feet from his friend Angela Potts's white sneakers. She stood there on the sidewalk frowning at him, purse in one hand and a Krispy Kreme box in the other.

"Get in," he said.

"Am I being arrested?"

He sighed. "You're always butting in, and this time I'm inviting you. Must you make everything difficult?"

"You smelled my donuts, didn't you."

On their way down the street he broke the news. Twenty minutes ago a man in a black ski mask had robbed the local bank and escaped in a purple car with Michigan plates. Shortly afterward, the sheriff's cousin

Mae Pender phoned to say a speeding car had stopped next door, and a strange man had hauled a garbage bag inside. No one had left the house since.

"Who lives next door?" Angela asked, chewing.

"A lady that Mae doesn't know. But she knows her neighborhood's cars, and this one didn't belong." He paused and added, "It's purple, with an out-of-state tag."

"Interesting. So you're checking it out."

"As much as possible, without a search warrant. No time for that. And since one deputy's sick and the other's out of town—"

"You need my help."

"Well, I need somebody to wait outside, and call dispatch if I run into trouble."

Angela thought that over. "No," she said.

"You won't help?"

She smiled. "I won't wait outside."

Ten minutes and three donuts later, they parked behind the possible getaway car. It indeed had Michigan plates. Together they crept to the house. Next door Mae Pender stuck her head out. The sheriff waved her back inside.

With one hand on his holstered gun, he reached for the doorbell—and paused. Someone inside was talking.

"Come on, Jeannie," a male voice said. "Let's go get a burger."

"I'd rather eat here." A female. "The Channel Five weatherman said a storm's coming."

"Lou Burnett? Burnett's been wrong a million times. The sun's shining."

"But we agreed to stay inside, Marty."

"Stop worrying. Nobody saw—"

The conversation stopped. On the porch, Angela and the sheriff held their breaths.

"What is it?" Jeannie's voice hissed.

"Somebody's here."

Too late, the sheriff realized his shadow was on the front window. Angela sighed, glared at him, and pushed the doorbell.

More silence, then footsteps. A wide-eyed woman—Jeannie?—opened the door.

The sheriff flashed his badge, asked for a walk-through, and confirmed that no one else was home. The living room was tiny: threadbare couch, old-fashioned television, lamp, and a smaller TV on an end table. The man—Martin Russell—said the car was his, and that he lived a thousand miles away, in Detroit. He looked calm. The woman seemed worried. The sheriff said, watching them, "I've asked for a warrant to search the house."

"Go ahead," Russell said.

"Excuse me?"

"Forget the warrant. Search away. We got nothing to hide."

The sheriff's heart sank. He'd heard the cool certainty in Russell's voice: a search would be fruitless. But Angela looked thoughtful. Suddenly she said, "I'd like to buy your TV."

Jeannie blinked. "What?"

"Your TV. The old one. I'll give you a thousand dollars."

"It doesn't even work."

"I don't care." Angela took out her checkbook. "How about two thousand?"

Both Jeannie and Russell were sweating now. Neither said a word.

"No? That's what I thought." Angela turned to the sheriff. "Arrest them both, Chunky."

Afterward, they discovered that Martin Russell had stolen a tourist's car and that he and Jeannie were planning a one-way trip to Mexico later this week. More importantly, when at Angela's suggestion the sheriff unscrewed the back of the ancient TV set, they found that its huge gutted interior contained the bank's missing cash and a black ski mask.

He shook his head, stunned. "I would never have thought to search there."

"They figured that. All I did was prove it had to be there."

"How'd you know to ask? Because she was nervous?"

"Because he was lying."

"But what clued you in? Something he said to us?"

She grinned. "Something he said to *her*."

MYSTERY:

What gave Martin Russell away?

9

PAR FOR THE COURSE

SHERIFF Charles Jones, blissfully alone on the seventh hole, drew back his club, swung hard—and barely touched the ball. It fell off the tee and rolled less than a foot.

"I know what you're doing wrong," a voice said, from behind him.

The sheriff turned to see Angela Potts, his former fifth-grade schoolteacher, standing beside his electric golf cart. He snorted and said, "What do *you* know about this sport?"

"I know I never saw anybody hit a ten-inch drive before. And I'm pretty good at it, actually."

He replaced the ball on the tee. "I'm on vacation, Ms.

Potts. What do you want?"

"A date with Hugh Jackman. What I *need* is for you to come with me."

"Because?"

"There's been a robbery."

Moments later they were gliding toward the clubhouse. "Nice cart," she said to him. "I heard your uncle Parnell goes to work in one of these things."

"He goes *everywhere* in one, as of yesterday. He sold his real car."

"Why?"

"He never drives far, so—" The sheriff paused, looking at her. "What's the matter?"

"Parnell's the reason I'm here," she said.

"You mean it was his house that was robbed?"

"Your aunt says he did the robbing."

Sheriff Jones shook his head. "What a family." He thought a minute, then said, "What *was* I doing wrong, on my golf swing?"

She smiled. "You stand too close to the ball . . ."

"I do?"

". . . after you hit it."

• • •

They found Wilma Jones on her porch, shelling peas in a dishpan. Recently divorced, her ex-husband Parnell now lived in a nearby motel. "But he occasionally sleeps here, on the couch," she said. "He did last night."

"What exactly was stolen?" the sheriff asked.

"My savings. More'n two thousand dollars."

"You're sure it was Uncle Par?"

"I'm sure. I'd already gone to bed, but I heard him come in around ten."

Angela frowned. "You heard him unlock the front door, you mean?"

"No, my bedroom's all the way in the back—I just heard him bumping around, inside. But what first woke me up was, I heard him pull into the driveway. Then this morning he was gone, along with my money." She stayed quiet awhile, her fingers expertly stripping the peas. "And yes, I keep the house locked. Parnell and Rollie are the only ones besides me who have a key, and Rollie's in the Army, down at Shelby."

Rollie Jones was their good-for-nothing son, and Camp Shelby was an army base two hundred miles south. "Can you picture Jolly Rollie in a uniform?" the sheriff murmured to Angela.

"What'd you say?" Wilma snapped.

"Nothing, Aunt Wilma."

"Anyhow, there's one piece of good news," she said. "The cash was marked."

"Marked?" Angela asked.

"I had put a little red mark on one corner of every bill. If you find Parnell, you'll find my money."

The sheriff and Angela exchanged a glance. "I'll find him," he said. "Anything else you can tell us?"

"Yeah. Before you go, be a good boy and fetch my electric fans down from the attic."

• • •

Back in the patrol car, the sheriff took off his hat and looked at Angela. "What are you grinning about?"

"While you were up in the attic I made a phone call to Moe's Tavern here in town," she said. "Remember how Rollie used to love to go to Moe's?"

"So?"

47

Her grin widened. "Rollie might be downstate playing soldier, but last night at eleven he was right here, at his old watering hole. A dozen people saw him there. And when I asked Moe to check his cash register—"

"Don't tell me. Red marks on the bills."

Angela nodded. "Apparently your cousin Rollie's even dumber than he used to be. Parnell, by the way, wasn't there."

Sheriff Jones let out a sigh of relief, then frowned. "But wait . . . how'd you figure it out?"

"Golf's not the only thing I'm good at," she said.

MYSTERY:
||||||||||||||||||||||||||||||||||||||||

What made Angela think Rollie Jones was guilty?

10

A ROOM FOR THREE

Retired schoolteacher Angela Potts strolled into Sheriff Jones's office to find him and Deputy Fred Prewitt staring at a TV screen.

"Who's playing?" she asked. "And who's ahead?"

The sheriff looked up. "The criminals are," he said. "That shooting, east of town—Claude Weaver? Yesterday a lady phoned and told me I'd soon know the killer's identity. Then this morning I found a DVD and audio tape on the front steps when I came in."

Deputy Prewitt hit a button on the DVD player; on the screen Angela saw three people entering a wooden shed, from different directions. Two men and a woman. Several minutes later, according to the on-screen timestamp, all three were shown leaving again. "Good view of their faces," Prewitt said. "The audio tape's a different matter, though—the quality's bad, so the male voices sound too much alike to differentiate between them. We can't tell who's who."

Angela studied the screen. "You're saying someone hid an audio recorder in there, and then secretly made this video?"

The sheriff nodded. "Yep. And I recognized the place—a little outbuilding near an abandoned farm on Summit Road. Prewitt and I drove there awhile ago. It has only the one door, and one window in the back. But there's a cliff right behind it."

"Why's the layout important?" she asked.

"Because we see three people enter and leave—but from what was said, there seem to be four people on the audio."

Angela blinked. "So—someone else was already in there, and stayed afterward?"

"Our first thought. But whoever videoed this walks to the shed after, and films the interior. Nobody's inside."

"A camera trick, maybe? An editing job?"

"No. We've watched it over and over."

"So, no matter what you heard, or think you heard, there must've been only three people present."

He shrugged. "You'd have to hear the audio, to see what I mean."

"Well, let's hear it then," she said.

"Play it, Fred," the sheriff said. Then, to Angela: "Pay special attention to the names they use."

Prewitt turned to a small cassette deck and pressed PLAY. The first sound was that of a creaky door. Then the following:

"Crazy place to meet," a man's voice said.

A female voice replied, "Better safe than sorry."

"I'm already sorry," a man said (the same man? It was impossible to tell). "This has turned into a—" He uttered a word, then added, "No offense, Reverend Barnes."

"You're worried about language?" a male voice asked. "You've just murdered someone."

"You weren't supposed to hurt anybody, Johnson," the woman agreed.

"I know. I was asking Weaver for the money, and my gun went off. Reverend, don't look at me that way—the fact is, it was an accident."

Male voice: "The fact is, you're a fool, Johnson. What do we do now?"

"We don't do anything. Nobody saw me."

"Where was your girlfriend?"

"Gone. We broke up."

"What do *you* hear, Tyler?" the woman said. "You're the one with the contacts."

"Nothing, so far. We're free and clear. Johnson's ditched the gun, and he's right, nobody knows he was there. We'll lay low a couple months, then try again."

"Not me," someone said. "I'm out."

"Nobody's out. We're all in this together."

"I wish I'd never met you idiots," the female voice said.

"You'd see it different if we were here to divide the loot. I told you, it was an accident."

"This meeting's over," someone said. "Let's go."

The sound of rusted doorhinges again—and then silence.

"Okay," the sheriff said, listening to the dead hiss

of the tape. "Here's what we know. Three people en-ter, three leave. A male named Johnson's the gunman. The woman addresses someone as Tyler, and there's a preacher named Barnes. Four people. I'm guessing the absent girlfriend is our spy." He looked at Angela and his deputy. "The men all sound the same—we can't match any faces and names. Is Johnson one of those we saw, or is he the missing suspect? And since there's no exit from the window, how could there even *be* a fourth suspect?"

"There wasn't," Angela said, smiling. "You'll prove that when you question the person I have in mind."

"Who is it?" the sheriff asked.

MYSTERY:

Which person had the face that Angela could match with a name?

11

LIAR, LIAR

Dʀᴇssᴇᴅ in her Sunday best, Angela Potts marched across the parking lot, dug her keys from her purse, and looked up to see the county sheriff leaning against her car. "Wonder of wonders," she said. "Chunky Jones, within a hundred yards of a church."

Sheriff Jones looked up at the cloudless summer sky, then down at the umbrella in her hand. "You expecting rain?"

"One never knows. It rained all day Friday."

"And was clear every other day for the past week."

Angela sighed. "Are you here to discuss the weather?"

"I'm here to ask if you're busy, after lunch."

"Why?"

"I'm meeting your cousin Pearl Hinson," he said, "to discuss her granddaughter's car accident."

"And you want me along?"

"At Pearl's request. She doesn't like me much."

"Well, this'll even things out," Angela said, adjusting her hat. "I don't like Pearl much either."

"Just don't call me Chunky," he said.

During lunch at Wendy's, the sheriff filled her in. Local farmer John Adkins had recently called to report that someone had crashed a car into his tractor, which he'd left parked beside a dirt road near his farm. The only evidence was blue paint on the mangled tractor, and the mangled front bumper of a car. There were no witnesses—Adkins lived two miles from town—but on a routine patrol yesterday afternoon, Deputy Fred Prewitt spotted a wrecked blue Lexus outside a repair shop. The car, minus its front bumper, was traced to sixteen-year-old Laura Hinson. The Hinsons had made a day-trip to Memphis yesterday but agreed to meet with the sheriff today.

Angela and Sheriff Jones found Laura, her parents, and her grandmother Pearl waiting for them in Pearl's living room. In case it wasn't already clear, Pearl started off by letting everyone know who was boss.

"What are you planning to do, Sheriff?" she snapped.

"I plan to get a statement from your granddaughter. I already have one from Mr. Adkins, who says his tractor was damaged while sitting unattended and safely off the roadway."

All heads turned to young Laura, who didn't appear at all flustered. In fact she looked incredibly bored.

"It was so *not* off the road," she said. "I knocked it off when I hit it. It was like totally *in* the road."

"Adkins says it was parked well onto the shoulder," the sheriff said, "where he always leaves it."

Laura shrugged. "Liar, liar, pants on fire."

"Let's say it *was* in the road. You couldn't go around it?"

"I couldn't even *see* it. I had just met a car coming my way, and it had raised a cloud of dust."

The sheriff frowned. "And the tractor was parked in your lane?"

"*Lane?* Duh—there weren't any lanes, or any lines. It's a dirt road. But yes, it was on my side."

"If that's true, Laura, why didn't anyone else report it?"

"Don't be stupid, Sheriff," Pearl Hinson said, with an eye-roll. "Nobody travels that horrible road."

"Laura did, and apparently somebody else did too, if she met a car going the opposite direction."

"Are you accusing me of reckless driving?" Laura asked.

The sheriff did a palms-up. "I'm just trying to find out what happened."

She raised her chin. "What happened was, the tractor was in my way and I hit it because I couldn't see it for the dust. I was like, what's *that* doing here?"

"Laura was taking a shortcut to the club," Pearl explained. "Thank goodness she wasn't injured."

"The club?"

"Hillside Country Club," she said, raising her chin exactly as Laura had done. It reminded Angela why she'd never been fond of Cousin Pearl.

The sheriff asked Laura, "What time was the accident?"

She shrugged. "Around noon."

"Yesterday?"

"Day before yesterday." Her nose wrinkled in distaste. "Only *working people* go to the club on weekends."

Angela thought: Not any working people *I* know.

"Why didn't you report this, Laura?" the sheriff asked.

Another shrug. "Why bother? Daddy said he'd fix the car."

The sheriff jotted some notes and turned to Angela. "You have anything to add?"

"Just one thing," she said. "Laura, darling? You're guilty as sin."

MYSTERY:
||||||||||||||||||||||||||||||||||||

What convinced Angela that Laura Hinson was the one who was lying?

12

THE PRESIDENT'S RESIDENCE

On Monday at noon Sheriff Chunky Jones got two unpleasant surprises at the same time. First, his old schoolteacher Angela Potts barged into his office; second, Deputy Fred Prewitt called from his cruiser.

"Something's up," Prewitt said. "That state cop, the one who doesn't like you—"

"Bradshaw?"

"He's here. I spotted him coming into town and followed him. He made one stop at the college, then drove across campus and parked in front of the White House."

The sheriff frowned, thinking. The White House was the home of the president of the small community college here in town. It was also, at the moment, vacant.

Its most recent resident had quit in May for a better position upstate.

"I'm on my way," the sheriff said, and hung up.

"We," Angela corrected. "*We're* on our way."

They walked outside, where he took a cigar from his pocket. "You won't mind if I smoke this in the car, right?"

"Just don't exhale," she said.

Their smokeless trip took twelve minutes. They arrived to find Deputy Prewitt parked at the head of a driveway leading into the woods at the edge of the campus. Barely visible through the pines was a large white house and a large black car.

"Has he seen you?" Sheriff Jones asked him.

"Bradshaw? No. Just seems to be watching the house."

The sheriff and Angela drove on and parked beside Officer Bradshaw, who climbed out of his car. "Well, well," he said. "Fatman and Robin."

"You didn't tell me you were coming," the sheriff said.

"I'm on a case. Plus, I didn't want you trying to tell me how to do my job."

"Somebody needs to," Angela said. "Our deputy just followed you three miles without your even seeing him."

Before Bradshaw could reply, the sheriff asked, "What case?"

Bradshaw hesitated, then said, "We got a call saying Fruity Lassiter's using this house as a hideout."

"Lassiter? The racketeer? I thought he was in prison."

"He escaped, three weeks ago. But I'm thinking the caller was mistaken. I stopped by Campus Security to pick up the door key, and they said they check on the house every Monday morning and that nobody else has been down this driveway in months. Just wanted to see for myself."

"We'll go with you," Angela said.

"Must be my lucky day." Bradshaw climbed the porch steps, unlocked the front door, and entered the house. Angela and the sheriff followed.

They saw nothing suspicious. The electricity and gas were turned off, the beds made, sink empty, bathrooms clean, closets bare. The place was quiet except for the steady ticking of an antique clock. "Nobody's staying here," Bradshaw said. "This is a waste of time." Without another word, he stalked out to his car and drove away.

Angela said, as she and Sheriff Jones watched him leave, "Isn't there an old log road through the woods near here?"

"Just behind the house."

She smiled. "Want to be a hero?"

"What do you mean?"

"I'm thinking we should wait here awhile." She dug a miniature chess set out of her purse and pointed to the porch swing. "Have a seat."

"Chess?" he said.

"It's, like, checkers for smart people."

"I know how to play chess," he growled.

After twenty minutes and five checkmates by Angela, they heard the rumble of an approaching motor. One peek around the back corner revealed a ratty-looking guy on an ATV bumping toward them on the logging road.

Fruity Lassiter spotted them too late to run. Within minutes he was handcuffed and loaded into the patrol car.

"How did you know, Ms. Potts?" the sheriff asked.

"Campus Security isn't exactly NYPD. I bet they

just check to make sure the lights are off and the windows aren't broken. Besides, Lassiter would know their schedule, and probably cleans everything up and leaves before they come around. Like he did today."

"And picks the lock?"

"Probably."

"But how'd you figure he was here at all?"

Angela smiled. "Because he made a mistake."

MYSTERY:

What made Angela think somebody was currently living in the house?

13

A QUICK STOP

"UNSCHEDULED layover," Sheriff Jones announced. "Driver needs potato chips."

Angela Potts sighed from the passenger seat. "Do you ever eat anything besides junk food?"

"Sure I do. I eat donuts." He steered his cruiser into the gravel lot of Joe Garcia's Quik Stop and cut the engine. "Sorry, Ms. Potts—when your car's broken and you're bumming a ride home from your sewing circle, you don't get to make the rules."

"Rules? Here's a rule. Students should be polite to their former teachers."

The sheriff didn't reply; he was already out and headed for the store. Grumbling, Angela climbed out too, and followed. The building glowed in the setting sun, and she could hear ducks quacking in the creek behind it.

Then they stopped in their tracks.

Two men lay dead behind the gas pumps. Each held a pistol. Standing beside them was a wide-eyed young man in muddy shoes.

The sheriff drew his gun. "What happened here?"

"They shot each other," the man blurted. "About a minute ago."

Sheriff Jones studied the bodies. One was Big Joe Garcia, the owner. The other was a small guy, middle-aged. "Who are you?" the sheriff asked the young man. "You know these people?"

"No. My name's Pete Crawford, I just got here. I walked—my Jeep's parked somewhere over the hill there, on the shoulder of the interstate." He pointed a trembling finger across the dirt road.

Sure enough, only three cars were here. Garcia's, the sheriff's, and an unfamiliar SUV. The sheriff noted its Louisiana plates: everyone knew Garcia had gambling debts in New Orleans. He steered Crawford into the building and patted him down—he was unarmed—while Angela called to report the shooting.

Afterward, she turned to Crawford. "You said you walked here?"

"Yes ma'am. I ran out of gas, on the interstate." He swallowed. "I was on my way to Atlanta from Texas Tech, and was gonna get off here to fill up but I missed the exit ramp—the sun was in my eyes. Then I spotted this, above the trees off to the right"—he pointed to the tall Exxon sign outside—"just as my Jeep died."

"Where's your gas can?"

"I was hoping to buy one here." His voice was shaking.

"Can I go now?"

"No," Angela said. She pulled the sheriff aside and whispered, "Question: What would you do if you had a gun, and this had just happened, and you saw a sheriff's cruiser coming? And there's no place to hide."

He blinked. "You think he had a gun?"

"You'd get rid of it," she answered. "Right? And how would you do that?"

Sheriff Jones stared at her. "I don't know—"

"You'd throw it in that creek out back. See the mud on his shoes?"

"He could've gotten muddy walking here from the interstate."

Angela shook her head. "That's high ground, and dry. I don't think he walked here at all."

The sheriff frowned. "So—you think he came here with this other dead guy? In the SUV?"

"I think so. Would *you* have come alone, to settle a debt with a guy the size of Big Joe Garcia?"

Angela's phone buzzed. She turned away and took the call. Moments later she disconnected and walked over to Crawford. "That was Deputy Fred Prewitt. He was on his way here, so I asked him to detour and check on your abandoned Jeep. Want to guess what he found?"

Pete Crawford's shoulders slumped.

"He said there's no car parked beside the interstate, Mr. Crawford. What do you think of that?"

Suddenly he turned and dashed to the door—and ran straight into a surprised Deputy Prewitt, who grabbed him and held on.

"Anything you want to tell us, Mr. Crawford?" Angela asked.

Struggling, Crawford wailed, "He wouldn't pay us.

We warned him." Within seconds he was handcuffed and led away.

Stunned, the sheriff turned to Angela. "You knew he was involved?"

"Only because he lied."

"Wait a minute. If Prewitt's *here*—who phoned you just now?"

"The repair shop. My car's ready."

"So you were bluffing?"

"Why not?" she said. "He was bluffing *us*."

MYSTERY:

|||||||||||||||||||||||||||||||||

*Which of Crawford's lies first made
Angela suspicious?*

14

IN OTHER WORDS

"Ms. Potts?" said the voice on the phone. "This is Sheriff Jones. I have some interesting news."

Retired teacher and amateur crime crusader Angela Potts switched the light on and checked her bedside clock. 11:40 p.m. "Where are you?"

"Parked in your driveway."

"Have I won the state lottery?" she asked.

"No."

"Does George Clooney need a date for the Oscar ceremony, and hasn't been able to reach me?"

"No . . ."

"Then it can wait. Have a nice—"

"There's been a murder," the sheriff said. "And looks

like the victim left a note about the killer."

A long silence passed.

"I'll need coffee," she said.

"Got it right here."

Ten minutes later the two of them arrived at the mansion of retired senator Arlington Hill. A tearful private nurse, Ms. Larkin, led them upstairs to his study, where Hill's body lay slumped in his desk chair. A Scrabble board was on the broad desktop, and scattered letter-tiles were the only hint that there'd been a struggle. "We were in the middle of a game," the nurse explained, wiping her eyes, "when he sent me down to the all-night market for peanuts. He loved roasted peanuts."

"You found him like this when you got back?"

"Yes sir."

The sheriff leaned over to study the old man's body. He had stab wounds in his chest. On the desk in front of him, amidst the scattered tiles, was a neat string of letters. They spelled out the words NIECE DID IT.

"This is the 'note' you told me about, on the phone?"

The nurse nodded. "He must've lived just long enough to gather those letters and arrange them that way. I was careful not to touch anything."

"Which niece?" Angela said. "Didn't he have two?"

"Yes. His late brother's daughters, Mary and Edith. His only remaining relatives. They live here, and are downstairs, resting—I gave them mild sedatives."

"What did they say about what happened?" the sheriff asked.

"Nothing. When I told them about his death, both were distraught. Neither one came in here with me, so they haven't seen the message he left."

"If the message is correct, Ms. Larkin, one of them

did come in here," he said. "While you were gone."

The nurse nodded, still sniffling. She didn't seem to realize that she could be a suspect too—but Angela doubted she was guilty. A private nurse for an old and wealthy bachelor was probably a dream job, and she'd have nothing to gain from Senator Hill's early demise. The nieces, on the other hand . . .

"I assume his entire estate goes to them?" Angela asked.

"Yes—it's in his will."

"Both are single, right?"

"Yes. Edith never married; Mary divorced years ago, but kept her married name—Brooks.

"Could you wake them?" the sheriff said. "For questioning?"

"Yessir. I'll bring them up." The nurse scurried away, leaving Angela and the sheriff alone.

"What do you think?" he asked.

Angela studied the incriminating "message," then the rows of books on the walls of the study. "I think it's what it looks like. Those bookshelves are full of mystery novels. I think he gave us a dying clue to the identity of his murderer. Pretty clever."

"But if one of the nieces did it, they'd still have to split the assets."

"So? Fifty percent of a fortune's better than a hundred percent of nothing."

"Good point," he said. "But you're forgetting something—why didn't he just spell out the name? Why be vague, and say 'niece'?"

"Because that was all he could do."

"What?"

She pointed. "He had only those letters in the

message, plus two U's, an H, a W, and a couple of P's. All the other letters are on the table, but were too far away to reach."

"But . . . which niece is guilty?"

"Mary," Angela said.

He stared at her. "How do you know?"

"Because I'm pretty clever myself."

MYSTERY:

*How **did** Angela know which niece was guilty?*

15

HIGHWAY ROBBERY

An hour before sundown, retired schoolteacher Angela Potts was the only customer at Hazel Reeves's Texaco station, on Highway 18. Angela stood there pumping gas into her soon-to-be-antique Buick and muttering as she watched the meter tick off the dollars.

"Shame on you, Angel," Hazel called, walking past. "Did I hear you say 'highway robbery'?"

"How would I know?"

"How would you know if you said it?"

"How would I know if you heard me?" Angela shut off the pump, hung up the nozzle, fetched her purse from inside the car, and was giving the meter another dark look when she heard something herself: three loud

POPs from the other side of the building. She and Hazel exchanged a surprised glance, then hurried around the corner.

There was no one in sight. Just a white car that said HARRELSON VENDING CO. on the door, parked under a shade tree on the far side of Hazel's lot. Beyond it was a grassy slope leading down to the river.

Angela approached the car, crept around it—and stifled a scream. The driver's side door was open, and on the ground beside it lay a middle-aged man in a pool of blood. She whipped out her cell phone and punched in 911. Hazel leaned over him and said, wide-eyed, "He's still breathing."

Angela finished the call, disconnected, and knelt beside the man. Gently she pried a pistol loose from his right hand, and when she did he opened his eyes and looked dazedly up at her. His face was pale and sweaty.

"Want some water, Mister?" she whispered.

He seemed to focus on her. "Might," he said, and with a shaky finger pointed toward the grassy slope.

She nodded. "Well, I just might have some. And no, I won't have to go down to the river to get it." She opened her giant purse and removed a plastic bottle—but before she could unscrew the cap, he passed out again.

Within moments an ambulance arrived, followed by Sheriff Charles Jones, and five minutes later the injured man was whisked away to the hospital. Angela showed the sheriff the gun and updated him on what she and Hazel had found.

"That's all he said?" Sheriff Jones asked. "The word 'might'?"

Angela nodded. "That's it."

"Looks like he fired one round."

"And we heard three shots."

"No suicide attempt, then." The sheriff thought a moment. "Did either of you recognize him?"

"I did," Hazel said. "Name's Russell Brown. He's only been here a couple months."

"In town, you mean?"

"In this country. He's from Australia. Told me he ran a courier service in Sydney." Hazel squinted, remembering. "He and his business partner—a guy named Sam Pierce—went bust, Brown said, and moved here because Pierce has elderly relatives nearby. They both hired on as drivers with Jeeter Harrelson's company but Pierce was fired several weeks ago. Brown told me he hadn't seen his friend since then. Every afternoon around this time, Brown stops here, buys a Pepsi from me, drinks it sitting over there in the shade, and then leaves to deliver the day's proceeds."

"Proceeds from what?"

"Vending machines," Hazel said. "He gathers the cash from all the Harrelson locations and keeps it in a metal strongbox on the back seat—" She paused. The same thought seemed to have struck all of them at the same time. When they looked, sure enough, the car's rear seat was empty.

"Okay," the sheriff said. "Armed robbery, then. Ladies, don't touch anything else. I'm headed back to—"

He stopped as Angela turned and marched off down the weedy slope toward the river. "Ms. Potts?"

"He pointed this way," she called, over her shoulder.

She kept walking, and when the sheriff and Hazel followed they found her standing at the water's edge, staring at a beached motorboat. Lying face-down in the boat was a dead body in a bloody shirt, and beside it a

.38 revolver and an overturned steel cashbox.

"The armed robber," Angela said.

The sheriff checked the man's pockets and sighed. "No ID."

"Doesn't matter," she said. "He's Sam Pierce."

MYSTERY:
‖‖‖‖‖‖‖‖‖‖‖‖‖‖‖‖‖‖‖‖‖‖‖‖‖‖‖‖‖‖‖‖‖

Why did Angela think the thief was
Russell Brown's former partner?

16

A DIRTY TRICK

SHERIFF Jones was in a grumpy mood. His head ached, he was freezing, and it was Monday morning. To make matters even worse, the first person he saw when he arrived at Clarkson's Cleaners was his bossy former schoolteacher, Angela Potts.

"Did my dispatcher tip you off?" he asked, as he slammed his car door.

Angela was climbing out of her old Buick. "What?"

"Answer my question, Ms. Potts. How else could you show up so fast at the scene of every crime? Do you think I'm stupid?"

"That's two questions," she said.

"I mean it—why are you here?"

"To drop off my dry cleaning, you moron." She held up an armload of clothes. "The scene of what crime?"

Instead of answering, he marched past her and through the door. Angela followed him.

Betty Clarkson, her face drawn and pale, was behind the counter. "Thanks for coming, Sheriff."

"What happened, Ms. Clarkson?"

She swallowed. "A tall guy came in. Coat, cap, a scarf wrapped around his face. It's so cold I wasn't suspicious of that—but then he robbed me."

The sheriff took out a notebook and pen. "How much?"

"All last week's cash. Three thousand dollars. I always wait till Mondays to take it to the bank, because Friday afternoons are so busy. And I was here alone today—my husband Dwayne's home with the flu."

Angela, still holding her bundle of clothes, said, "Any idea who it was?"

"Yes—a bum I've seen on the street. He asked me last week for bus fare."

"I thought you said his face was covered."

"It was." Betty Clarkson patted the back of her left hand. "But he has a tattoo of an eagle, right here. I recognized it."

Then something caught Angela's eye: a tiny, wall-mounted surveillance camera, aimed right at them. "Was that turned on?" she asked, pointing.

Betty nodded. "Still is. Want to see the tape?"

Angela and the sheriff spent the next ten minutes alone and shivering in the shop's chilly office, watching a VCR replay of the robbery. The suspect was indeed bundled up in coat, gloves, cap, and scarf, and had been inside only for a moment. They couldn't see his eyes; his face was turned away the entire time. Betty Clarkson promptly handed him a huge money pouch, then he fled the scene.

"I'll be right back, Chunky." Angela stood and picked up a phone book. "I need to make a call."

"Did you spot something?" the sheriff asked.

"Keep looking. Watch him when he enters and leaves."

"Don't call me Chunky," he called after her.

She returned a moment later, pocketing her cell phone. "Notice anything?"

The sheriff pointed to the screen. "His head's way below the top of the door. He's not tall like Ms. Clarkson said. He's short."

"Right. So is her husband."

"What?"

"That camera's not easy to see," Angela said. "This guy already knew it was there, and looked the other way. And why was she so quick to hand over last week's money? She could've just given him what was in the register—a street bum wouldn't have known any different." She paused. "I remember Dwayne Clarkson—he served five years for fraud. I'm betting they faked the robbery and invented a suspect. They keep the cash, insurance covers the 'loss.'"

The sheriff thought that over. "What if he really *is* home sick?"

"Dwayne? He's home, but not sick. He's just dumb."

"What?"

"I called their house just now," Angela said, "and told him the electronics store next door is giving away free TVs until ten o'clock. He's on his way there now—and he sounded healthy to me."

"I believe I'll have a word with him, when he arrives."

"We might also want to compare what he's wearing to

what we just saw here, on the tape."

The sheriff studied her a moment. "How did you figure it out?"

Angela nodded toward the front of the store. "Remember what she told us?"

"What about it?"

Angela gave him a sly look. "The cleaning lady didn't come clean."

MYSTERY:

How did Angela know Betty Clarkson was lying?

17

THE RULES OF THE GAME

SHERIFF Jones found Angela Potts kneeling in her flower garden beside her house. When she looked up at him the streaks of mud on her face reminded him of war paint, but he decided not to point that out.

"I need your advice, Ms. Potts," he said instead.

She wiped dirt from her forehead with a dirty glove, which didn't do a lot of good. "Say it one more time," she said.

He heaved a sigh. "I need your advice."

She grinned. "I like the sound of that."

His story took five minutes. His wife's niece Brittany Morgan had accused a local high school baseball player, Kevin Bassett, of stealing and pawning the wristwatch her parents had given her for her seventeenth birthday. Brittany had identified the thief, and so had the pawn-shop owner.

"Arrest him, then," Angela said.

The sheriff let out another breath. "There's a problem."

"What problem?"

"I just found out Brittany and Kevin were dating," he said. "They broke up the night before the incident. And Kevin's family's wealthy—why would he steal a watch?" The sheriff shook his head. "The whole thing sounds suspicious."

"So you think your niece might be stretching the truth a little."

He felt a pang of sadness. "Yes. But I have no proof of that."

Angela rose to her feet and brushed her knees off. "What did Brittany see, exactly?"

"She says she'd just parked her car in the lot outside our ball field right after the game two weeks ago, when we played Starkville High. While the teams were leaving the field, Britt left her purse on her car's hood and leaned back inside to get her coat. When she looked up again, Kevin Bassett was standing there, going through her purse. He dropped it quick and ran off."

"Wait a minute. She's a senior, and this was a home game. She didn't go?"

"Said she doesn't like baseball much. She just drove over, afterward, to meet a friend there."

"And she's sure it was Kevin who grabbed her purse?"

"Positive," the sheriff said. "He was still in uniform, she said—dark jersey, with his name on it."

"She didn't chase him, or call the police?"

"Said she was too shocked. And she didn't know

anything was missing from her purse until later."

"Anyone else see this happen?"

"Nope. Her friend wasn't there yet."

Angela studied her muddy trowel. "Why was Brittany's watch in her purse?"

"She said it didn't go with her outfit that day."

"And what made you check the pawnshops?"

"Just a hunch. As it turned out, Eddie Taylor—he runs the one on East Main—remembered buying the watch, and ID'ed Kevin Bassett as the seller, from a picture I showed him in the yearbook. Kevin was wearing sunglasses and a baseball cap the whole time, Eddie told me."

"So why'd Brittany wait so long to report the theft?"

"Her brother Jack's a ballplayer too, and about Kevin's size—apparently she had to talk Jack out of confronting Kevin and taking matters into his own hands."

A silence passed. The sheriff heard crows cawing in the stand of pines beyond the garden.

"What do you think?" he asked her.

"I think you should ask Brittany's brother to put on dark glasses and a cap and have the pawnshop owner take a look at him."

The sheriff blinked. "You figure she set the whole thing up?"

"It makes sense. That way, she pins this on her ex-boyfriend *and* gets the money for her 'stolen' watch. If Kevin's the one who broke off their relationship"—Angela shook her head—"young ladies can be mean creatures, Chunky, when they've been wronged."

He thought that over. "I don't know, Ms. Potts. I need a firm *reason* not to arrest him."

She took off her gloves and was quiet for a minute.

Finally she grinned, and turned to look the sheriff in the eye.

"You have it already," she said. "Brittany was lying to you, when she described what happened that night."

"How do you know?"

Her smile widened. "I never played ball—but I know the rules."

MYSTERY:
||||||||||||||||||||||||||||||||||

Why did Angela think Kevin Bassett was innocent?

18

A COLD CASE

SHERIFF Charles Jones stood at the ship's rail, staring across the water at the icebergs and snowfields. He was a lucky man, he thought. After years of grumbling to his wife about her addiction to entering contests, he'd been forced to eat his words: she had won an Alaskan cruise, for two. He'd never been up here before, and he loved it.

Only one thing bothered him. Before leaving, he'd forgotten to confront insurance agent Willis Purdy, who had managed to amass about a gazillion parking tickets. Since the county needed the funds—and since Willis was a jerk anyway—the sheriff decided it might be a good idea to call and ask Deputy Fred Prewitt to either collect the fines or throw the wily Willis in the clink.

Marveling at the technology that would allow a cell phone signal in such a remote location, Sheriff Jones punched in the number, waited a moment—and received the first bad turn of his day.

"Sheriff's office—Angela Potts speaking."

"Ms. Potts? What are you doing there?"

"Sally's on break, and I'm filling in. How's the cruise?"

At least she wasn't calling herself a deputy, he thought. "Okay, I guess."

"Ports of call?"

He had to think hard to remember. "Ketchikan, Juneau, Glacier Bay."

"Why not the Caribbean?"

"No sweaty beaches and margaritas for me. I'm on a journey of discovery and illumination."

"Like Captain Cook."

"Who?"

"Never mind," she said. "What is it you want, Chunky? I'm busy."

He sighed. Angela Potts had been his schoolteacher, back when mammoths roamed the earth. Now she was mostly a mammoth pain in the posterior.

"Actually," he said, "I have some news." He hesitated, then forged ahead. He was too excited not to tell *someone*. "I'm going to buy some land, up here."

"What?"

"Land. Property."

Silence. Then: "You planning to move to Alaska?"

"No, no, it's just an investment. Ten acres, near Juneau."

"How did this happen?"

"I met a real estate guy, here on the boat."

"His office is in Juneau?" she asked.

"No, some town about a hundred miles south of there."

"Sitka?"

"Could be, I don't know. Anyhow, he said he drives to Juneau once a week."

Another silence. "Have you seen the land?"

"We're three days away—but I've seen pictures of it. There's a competitive offer, so I need to sign the papers tomorrow."

"Where's your wife?"

"In our room, asleep," he said. "I'm out on deck."

"She know about this?"

"I want it to be a surprise. Look, I need to leave a message for Prewitt, so—"

"Don't do it," Angela said.

"What?"

"Don't sign the papers."

"No offense, Ms. Potts, but I—"

"I remember you never listened to me in school, Chunky Jones, and you'd be smarter if you had—but you better listen now." She paused. "Don't do this. Check the Better Business Bureau, ask the security folks on the ship, whatever. Don't rush into this, blind."

The phone connection went quiet.

"Chunky? You there?"

"No, I got ate by a polar bear."

"Eaten," she said. "My other line's blinking, I have to go. Remember, don't buy the land."

"Wait, Ms. Potts, I need you to tell Prewitt—"

Too late. She was gone.

The sheriff put his phone away and let out another sigh.

• • •

When he called the office the following day, sure enough, Angela was there again, but at least she wasn't manning the switchboard. He asked Sally to connect them.

"You propping your feet on my desk?" he asked.

"I wiped them off first," Angela said. "What do you need?"

"I need to thank you."

"He was a crook, right? The realtor?"

"Apparently. Several of us asked about him. Turns out he's from Miami. The pictures were fake—someplace in Montana. He snuck off at the last port."

"And the Chunkyman gets to save his money for a rainy day."

"It's a rainy day today," he said. "How'd you know?"

"That it's raining?"

"How'd you know about the real estate guy?"

He could picture her grinning, four thousand miles away. "I taught geography," she said.

MYSTERY:

What made Angela suspect that the realtor wasn't on the level?

19

ANGELA'S TAXI

Sheriff Charles T. Jones mumbled, from the passenger seat, "This is a little embarrassing."

"Begging rides from your former schoolteacher?" At the wheel, Angela Potts took her eyes off the road long enough to look at him. "You should've thought of that before you messed up your car."

"It was a mechanical malfunction."

"It was a brain malfunction. You can't keep driving for a week after the oil light comes on."

"They don't make patrol cars like they used to," he said.

"You're right—they make 'em better than they used to." She braked for a stop sign and squinted into the rising sun. "Where's this Jeffrey Boone live, exactly?"

The sheriff checked his notes. "Three houses up, on the left."

"And he's Tim Arnold's business partner?"

"Silent partner," the sheriff said. "Arnold's sister told me he hadn't seen Boone in weeks."

Unless they'd seen each other last night, Angela thought. According to the reports, Tim Arnold had been murdered while eating a bedtime snack at home—a neighbor had heard a gunshot around ten p.m. but had seen no one. And since there were no signs of forced entry, the killer must have been someone Arnold knew. Who else could get invited into his kitchen late at night?

As Angela steered her Buick into Jeffrey Boone's driveway, the sheriff said, "You wait in the car—that okay with you?"

"This isn't a taxicab. If you leave me in the car, you walk back to your office. That okay with you?"

Grumbling, he trudged to the front door and rang the bell. Angela followed him. Two minutes later they were seated in Boone's living room. Boone looked sleepy, in a robe and pajamas.

The sheriff wasted no time. "Timothy Arnold was killed yesterday," he said, "at his home."

Boone's jaw dropped. "Tim?" He suddenly looked wide awake. "What happened? He was in perfect health."

"Until he got shot," the sheriff agreed. He took out a notepad. "Anything you can tell us?"

Jeffrey Boone blinked several times, then swallowed and focused. "What do you mean, 'tell you'? Am I a suspect?"

"Everyone's a suspect."

"Look," Boone said firmly. "I was right here at home

last night. I haven't seen or talked to Tim in at least a month."

The sheriff made no reply.

"You should be questioning his ex-wife," Boone said. "Marlene. She hated him, you know."

Angela said, "We know Arnold was divorced, Mr. Boone. And the sheriff spoke with his sister Helen just after the murder. Did he have other relatives?"

"No. Why?"

She stared at him. "I was just wondering who stands to inherit his share of your company."

Boone cleared his throat. "Well, actually, we were partners. Therefore, I'll get the company."

"And how about the arguments you had with Arnold awhile back? We heard those got pretty nasty."

The sheriff gawked at her; Boone's jaw dropped. "What?"

"Financial trouble, right? I heard threats were made."

Boone's forehead was shining with perspiration now. "Look, I don't know what you—"

"Ms. Potts?" the sheriff said quietly. "Could I speak with you outside?"

Ignoring him, Angela leaned forward. "Do you own a gun, Mr. Boone? We brought a search warrant."

Boone gasped, his eyes wild. "Wait," he cried. "You don't understand. Tim wanted to sell the company. After all the time we put into that business, all the *work*— he wanted to sell out." His voice trembled. "Don't you see? I had no choice."

During the silence that followed, a stunned Sheriff Jones handcuffed Jeffrey Boone, informed him of his rights, and called dispatch. Afterward, when he and Angela were alone, he asked, "Search warrant?"

She shrugged. "I knew he was guilty. Figured I'd push him a little."

"'Arguments'?" he said. "'Financial trouble'?"

"Every partnership has arguments. *And* money problems."

"But how'd you know he was the killer?"

She grinned. "Years of training."

"Training?"

"Tell me something, Chunky: What did you watch the most on TV, when you were a kid?"

He shrugged. "Ballgames, I guess. And maybe Westerns."

"I watched *Dragnet*," she said.

MYSTERY:

What convinced Angela that Jeffrey Boone was the murderer?

20

A WARM WELCOME

DEPUTY Fred Prewitt stopped his cruiser at the head of the long driveway. Sheriff Chunky Jones was in the passenger seat; retired schoolteacher Angela Potts sat in the back.

"That's it," Angela said, pointing. "Frank's grand-mother's house."

"You were teachers at the same time, right?" the sheriff asked. "Think she'll remember you?"

"Who knows? Cordelia's at least ninety, by now."

"So you two are about the same age?"

Angela gave the sheriff a dark look. Prewitt was try-ing not to grin.

"Do you clowns want my help or not?" Angela asked.

"Just kidding, Ms. Potts. Fred, drop us off and stay in the car. Park where you can watch the back door."

Five minutes later Cordelia Morrison answered their knock and stood squinting at them from her front doorway. "Why, Angel Potts—what a surprise," she said. "And Sheriff Hollister. Have you gained some weight?"

The sheriff's face reddened. "I'm Charles Jones, ma'am. Hollister retired eight years ago."

The old lady seemed not to have heard him. She invited them into the living room, took a seat in an overstuffed chair—on the table beside it were a teacup and a half-finished knitted potholder—and directed Angela to a second padded chair. The sheriff pulled up a footstool and sat.

"Do you know why we're here?" he asked.

Cordelia sighed. "You're looking for Frankie, probably. The warden called me this morning."

"Escaping from a state prison's a serious matter, Ms. Morrison."

"And you thought he might be here?"

The sheriff was about to answer when he noticed a strange look on Angela's face. She seemed deep in thought.

He turned back to Cordelia. "Or that you might know where he is," he said. Frank Morrison had committed almost every non-violent offense in the book, but he was still just a kid. And his grandmother's farmhouse was only ten miles from the prison.

"Well, I don't," she said simply.

Angela, who still looked oddly thoughtful, said, "Do you live here alone, Cordelia?"

"Goodness, yes. I don't even own a pet."

"And no one else is here right now? Not a maid, a

neighbor, anyone?"

"Just you and Sheriff Hollister."

"Jones," he said.

"You keep any guns here in the house?" Angela asked.

Cordelia smiled. "None that still work."

"And you were sitting right there, knitting, when you heard us knock?"

"And drinking my tea."

The sheriff rose and cleared his throat. "Well. Many thanks, Ms. Morrison. We better be going, Ms. Potts."

Angela stood also. "Good to see you again, Cordelia. We'll find our way out."

Outside on the porch Angela stopped and faced the sheriff. "Knock again," she said, "and ask to use her bathroom."

He frowned. "What? I don't need to use the bathroom."

"You're right. What you *need* to do is search every room, upstairs and down, while I distract her."

"Search for what?"

"Frank Morrison," she said. "He's here in the house."

"He's what!?"

"I don't think it's risky—Frank's never used a weapon in any of his crimes, and if he walked here he probably hasn't even had time to get hold of one. But you better be ready, just in case."

After a little more convincing on Angela's part and a lot more frowning on Sheriff Jones's, he rapped again on the door. Sure enough, ten minutes later he came back downstairs leading a handcuffed and embarrassed-looking Frank Morrison. "Hi, Miss Angel," Frank said sadly.

While the prisoner was escorted to the cruiser—a surprised Deputy Prewitt hurried out to meet them halfway—Angela lingered on the porch with Cordelia.

"Jail's where he belongs," the old woman said quietly. "I think even he knows it."

"The two of you were sitting there talking just before we arrived, weren't you," Angela said. "Why didn't you just tell us?"

"He's my grandson. I couldn't."

Angela studied her and asked, "Then why did you seat us where you did?"

Cordelia smiled. "Because I wondered if you were still as smart as you used to be."

Angela smiled too. "Never underestimate a former schoolteacher," she said.

MYSTERY:
‖‖‖‖‖‖‖‖‖‖‖‖‖‖‖‖‖‖‖‖‖‖‖‖‖‖‖‖‖‖‖

What made Angela think Frank Morrison was in the house?

21

THIS SEAT'S TAKEN

DEPUTY Fred Prewitt was sitting at the sheriff's desk eating his lunch when retired teacher Angela Potts strolled in.

"Where's Boss Hogg?" she asked.

"Gulfport. Training course."

"Hope he learns quicker than he used to." Angela dropped into a chair. "So you're the head Fred?"

"Until tomorrow."

"A big seat to fill," she said. "Pun intended."

He grinned and was about to reply when the intercom blared. It was Sally the Dispatcher. "Fred? Beatrice Cooper on line two."

Prewitt looked at Angela, who explained, "Bea's a

widow, lives west of town, past the prison."

He nodded his thanks, pushed line two, and turned the speaker on so Angela could hear also.

"Sheriff Jones?" a voice said.

"I'm his deputy. May I help you?"

"It's my neighbor, Susan Roswell. I think she's in trouble."

In a trembling voice Bea Cooper explained that the Roswells and their two children, ages two and four, lived just across the road. This morning Susan had driven the kids to kindergarten as usual while her husband drove his truck to his town job. In fact, Bea said, she'd looked out her window five minutes ago to see (1) Susan's green Honda Civic in the Roswell driveway, (2) Susan herself exiting her front door holding a cell phone to her ear, and (3) three men standing around staring into her car's windows. Susan was approaching from the opposite side and didn't see them, but they saw her, and stepped quickly into the dark garage.

Alarmed, Bea was about to shout a warning when her telephone rang, in the other room. *She's calling ME,* Bea thought—but when she answered, it wasn't Susan, it was Bea's cousin Willard, the assistant warden at the nearby prison.

"Prison?" Prewitt asked her.

"He was calling to warn me that three inmates had just escaped."

"*What?*"

"I doubt anyone's heard yet, except me," Bea's voice said.

"Were they wearing prison clothes? Jumpsuits?"

"No—but they could've changed, right?"

"Bea, this is Angela Potts. Deputy Prewitt and I have

you on speakerphone. What happened then?"

"Well, Willard hung up before I could say anything, so I ran back to the window—and everybody was gone. Susan, the three men, everybody. We're in the flats out here, you know—no trees, only our two houses—and *nobody* was in sight. Then I saw her car heading off to the west." She paused. "I think they took her, Angela. I think they forced her into her car and drove off."

A silence passed. Finally Prewitt said, "Ms. Cooper, you stay inside and lock your doors. Understand?"

"Yes."

"I'll get back to you."

He switched the phone off and, ignoring the intercom, shouted, "Sally, get me the warden at the prison." To Angela he said, "I better go out there."

She shook her head. "Bea lives fifteen miles away, Fred. There's a state trooper speaking at the high school today, and that's near her house. Call him instead."

"Good idea." He phoned the school, located the trooper, and gave him a description of Susan's car and the direction it was headed. As he hung up, Sally stuck her head through the door.

"Can't get the prison," she said. "All the lines are busy. What's going on?"

Suddenly Angela gasped.

"What?" Prewitt asked.

"Call that trooper back. Divert him to the Roswells' house instead." She took out her phone and punched in numbers. "Bea? Angela again. How long were you away from the window?"

"What?"

"How long were you out of sight of those men, and of Susan's car?"

"Not long. Maybe ten seconds."

Angela turned to Prewitt and murmured, as if to herself, "Not enough time to switch things out."

Prewitt frowned. "Switch what out?"

Into the phone she said, "Bea? Have you called Susan's cell phone?"

"Yep. I got a 'not in service' message. Not surprising—there's a dead zone just west of us."

"Well, keep trying. If you reach her—this is very important—tell her not to go back home."

Angela disconnected and looked at a confused Deputy Prewitt.

"What *is* going on, Ms. Potts?"

"Those three convicts," she said, "aren't in Susan Roswell's car. They're probably hiding at her house."

MYSTERY:

Why was Angela convinced the escapees hadn't carjacked Susan's Civic?

22

THE COVER-UP

Retired schoolteacher Angela Potts pushed through the door of Roscoe's Café, stomped over to Sheriff Charles Jones's table, and stood there looking at him. A checkered napkin was stuffed into his collar and his mouth was full.

"You're still eating? It's almost nine."

He finished chewing and swallowed. "Six jumbo pancakes take awhile."

"Six?! And eggs and sausages too?"

"I'm on the Fatkins Diet. Earl Fatkins says, eat what tastes good and clean your plate."

"Well, Earl was wrong this time. Come with me."

"Why?"

"There's been a kidnapping." She marched toward the door. "Leave the napkin."

• • •

Angela briefed him as they drove to Elmer Liggett's house. Elmer's teenaged daughter Jenny had come home saying she'd been abducted from her car yesterday morning five miles north of town, on her way to visit her aunt Harriet. She'd been held by the kidnappers all day, but managed to escape during the night. Her mother had phoned Angela.

They arrived to find Jenny looking scared but unhurt, and flanked by both parents.

"Jenny," Sheriff Jones said to her, when they'd settled in, "can you identify your kidnappers?"

"No sir. It was just two men. They kept red handkerchiefs tied around their noses and mouths."

"Where'd they take you?"

She shrugged. "A shack in the woods. They blindfolded me for the trip there and back—I never even saw their car."

"How'd you get away?" Angela asked.

"I got myself untied, and climbed out a window."

"You did see the house, then?"

Jenny shook her blond head. "It was dark, and I never looked back. I found a road, and a trucker stopped for me. I asked him to take me to my car, then I drove home."

"You didn't tell him what happened?"

"I was too scared." She looked ready to cry.

The sheriff said, "They never hurt you, these men? Threatened you? Never made a ransom demand?"

"No sir."

"Did you recognize their voices?"

"No. All I remember"—she shivered—"is that one had big ears, and a black crewcut and mustache. The other was tall, with greenish eyes."

"Well, that's a start." He turned to her mother. "Didn't her Aunt Harriet call to tell you Jenny didn't arrive?"

Hilda Liggett shook her head. "Harriet wasn't expecting her, and doesn't have a phone anyway. Jenny had a cell phone, acourse, but there's no reception way out there."

Angela thought a moment, then asked Jenny, "Did you hear about yesterday's bank robbery down in Hattiesburg?"

"No ma'am. Why?"

"TV said it was a big guy and a short girl, with black ski masks and"—Angela glanced out the window at the driveway—"an old blue car. The girl had blond hair sticking out the bottom of her mask."

Jenny swallowed. "So?"

"Your boyfriend, Luke Branson—he still go to school down there?"

The sheriff cleared his throat. "Ms. Potts, what are you—"

"How far is it to Hattiesburg, Chunky?" Angela asked, still looking at Jenny. "Two hundred miles?"

"What exactly are you saying?" the sheriff said. Everybody was gaping at her.

"I'm saying I saw Jenny's car at Woody's Garage day before yesterday, getting serviced. And Woody always records the mileage." Angela paused. "If we check your car's odometer right now, Jenny, would it say it's traveled only ten miles since then? Or would it say four hundred?"

Jenny's cheeks had gone pale.

"And what would we find if we searched your car? Or your room? A black ski mask? Stolen cash?" Angela leaned closer. "Or does Luke have it?"

Jenny didn't answer. Angela looked her in the eye and said, "There was no kidnapping, was there. You just needed an alibi."

Jenny hesitated—then her face crumpled. "Luke and I want to get married," she blurted, "and we're both broke. He's the one who planned it . . ."

Later, after Jenny had been arrested and booked, the sheriff said to Angela, "How'd you know she was lying, about being kidnapped?"

"You'd have known too," she said, "if you'd listened."

MYSTERY:
||||||||||||||||||||||||||||||||||

What tipped Angela off?

23

OLLIE'S FOLLY

Retired schoolteacher Angela Potts was watering the rosebushes beside her mailbox when Sheriff Jones drove up. He said, through his open window, "Knock, knock."

She sighed. "Who's there?"

"Emerson."

"Emerson who?"

"Emerson fine flowers you got there."

She couldn't help grinning. Everyone in town knew by now that her roses had won the state Garden Club award.

"Congratulations," he added. "Heard first prize was five hundred bucks."

"Shopping, here I come." Angela studied him. "Why exactly are you here?"

"Sally has to babysit her grandson tomorrow—can you help with Dispatch?"

"Aha. *That's* why you're being so nice."

Before he could reply, his radio beeped. Sally's metallic voice said, "Possible burglar at Elsie Campbell's home, Sheriff. She's at work, and neighbor Maude Owen heard a noise coming from the house." The sheriff thanked her and disconnected.

"That's possible," Angela agreed. "Maude's bedridden, and her window's barely ten feet from Elsie's house. And Elsie sometimes leaves doors unlocked."

"Hop in," he said.

The drive took three minutes. As they arrived, a teenaged boy stepped down off Elsie Campbell's front porch. The sheriff jumped out, followed by Angela, and confronted him.

"What's your name, young man?"

"Oliver Mayfield." The kid looked terrified. "Ollie."

"Why aren't you in school?"

"It's Saturday."

Angela hid a smile; the sheriff blushed and said, "What were you doing in that house?"

"I wasn't *in* the house. I knocked—nobody's home."

"Why were you *at* the house?"

The boy pulled out a roll of cardboard tickets. "Selling raffle tickets. Eighth grade."

The sheriff studied him a moment. "You come with us."

Together they climbed the porch steps. Sheriff Jones knocked, called Elsie's name, waited, then entered through the (sure enough) unlocked front door. The others followed. A long hallway greeted them, with closed doors lining both sides. The house was dead silent.

"What's going on?" Ollie asked, his voice shaky.

"Neighbor heard a noise," the sheriff said. "You stick close to—"

"Whoa, I just heard something too," the kid whispered. He pointed to the third door on the right. "There—the kitchen."

The three of them crept down the hall.

The sheriff drew his pistol, carefully turned the knob, and threw open the door—

To reveal a gray cat sitting on a refrigerator. On the floor were two framed photos and a broken vase.

"So much for Maude's noises." The sheriff holstered his gun. "I owe you an apology, son."

At that moment his cell phone rang. He walked out to take the call, leaving Ollie and Angela in the kitchen.

The boy was still trembling. Angela stared at him.

"What?" Ollie said.

"What did you steal?" she asked quietly.

His eyes widened. "I didn't—"

"Let's see your pockets."

He hesitated, then his face and shoulders sagged.

Slowly Ollie surrendered his loot. Inside his baggy jacket were half a dozen packages of chicken and ground beef.

"What's this for?" she asked. But she thought she knew. She remembered seeing the name Mayfield while volunteering yesterday at the hospital.

"My family," he said, tears shining in his eyes. "Mom's sick, and Dad lost his job. When I walked by and saw this lady leave her house, and nobody was watching . . . I decided to jimmy the door."

"And found it unlocked."

"Yes, ma'am."

A silence passed. "Put the food back, Ollie. You know you have to."

He swallowed and nodded. When that was done, she added, "That was pretty smart, pointing out the cat. You saw it here earlier?"

"Yes ma'am."

"What's with the raffle tickets?"

"They're my older sister's."

Angela smiled. "That was pretty smart, too."

More silence. Finally he asked, "How did you know?"

Approaching footsteps interrupted them. "You two want a ride home?" the sheriff said.

"You go on ahead, Chunky. I think we're gonna stroll down to the corner."

"How about Dispatch, tomorrow?"

"I'll be there."

Outside, after the sheriff had driven away, Ollie said, "What's on the corner?"

"A supermarket. Follow me."

"Why?"

She smiled again. "We're going shopping."

MYSTERY:

||||||||||||||||||||||||||||||||||||||||

How did Angela know that Ollie Mayfield had been in the house?

24

THE TRUTH STINGS

SHERIFF Charles Jones was leaning against his cruiser in Cora Stewart's driveway when his former schoolteacher, Angela Potts, arrived. He looked down at his watch and said, "Finally."

"Sorry I'm late." She climbed out of her car. "I was at the beauty parlor."

"Looks like they didn't quite get finished," he said.

"Don't try to be witty, okay? Why'd you call me?"

"There was an incident here last night." He pointed to the Stewart house. "I need to question the daughter. Marge."

"Why do you need *me?*"

"For leverage. You know her, and she doesn't seem to

like me."

"Hard to imagine," Angela said. "All right, fill me in."

The sheriff glanced at his notepad. "Around midnight, when Marge and her boyfriend—Justin Perry—were pulling into her driveway here, somebody shot him."

Angela blinked. "What?"

"Somebody shot Perry dead, through the driver's-side window. Marge jumped out and took off through the woods, the shooter followed her, and she got away. She's okay, her mother said, except for some cuts from the windowglass."

"Good grief. How'd she escape?"

"Apparently she was trying to hide behind a tree, over there"—the sheriff pointed again—"but the killer saw her and was coming toward her with a flashlight, shining it right at her. It was pitch dark—no moon—but I'm told Marge knows every inch of these woods, and when the guy walked near a big nest of wasps between him and her, she threw her shoe into the nest."

"She *what?*"

"She's pretty smart. She knew the nest was there, she knew that in the dark the wasps would head straight for the light, and they did. The killer ran off screaming, and Marge ran to the house and locked herself in. She didn't realize until then that she'd been hurt."

"So what do you need to ask her?" Angela said.

"The name of the killer. She told her mother she recognized him."

Two minutes later Angela and the sheriff were sitting in Cora Stewart's living room, facing her and her daughter. Marge's left shoulder was bandaged.

The murderer, Marge told them calmly, was her ex-husband Dooley Watson. She had seen and recognized his face as he approached her in the woods with the flashlight. Just before the wasp attack.

Immediately Sheriff Jones phoned his office. "You know who Dooley Watson is?" he asked Deputy Prewitt. "Good. Bring him in."

When they were outside again, and alone, Angela turned to the sheriff. "She's wrong, Chunky."

"About what?"

"Dooley wouldn't hurt a fly. Besides, he still loves her."

"You heard what she said she saw, Ms. Potts."

"No, I heard what she *thought* she saw. Marge has also always thought Dooley was jealous."

"We'll leave that to the judge," he said. "Now, if you'll—"

"You know who this sounds like, Chunky? It sounds like Alvin Hollis."

The sheriff stared at her. "Al Hollis? The payroll thief?"

Angela nodded. "He vowed revenge, remember? It was Justin Perry's testimony that put him away."

"That's my point—Hollis is in prison."

"Not anymore. My cousin Bonnie knows his wife. She said Al's out on parole, as of yesterday."

Silence. "Does Marge know this?"

"Nobody here does."

The sheriff stewed a moment, then said, "That doesn't matter. She identified Dooley, and—"

"Wait," Angela said, holding up a forefinger. "Ten minutes. Give me ten minutes, right now, and I can solve this."

"What could you possibly do—"

"Let me try," she said. "Okay?"

The sheriff sighed. Angela whipped out her cell phone and started making calls.

Nine minutes later she disconnected and said, "I just talked to Al Hollis's wife. He's at home."

"So?"

"Now it's your turn," she said. "Call your deputy and see if he has Dooley Watson in custody yet."

"I would hope so—Dooley works two doors down from our office."

"Check and see. Ask how Dooley's doing. How he looks."

The sheriff made the call. Moments later he said to Angela, "He's already locked up. He's fine."

"Hollis isn't," she said, smiling.

"What do you mean?"

"His wife says he's covered with wasp stings."

MYSTERY:

Why did Angela suspect that Marge had mis-identified the killer?

25

TURN RIGHT
AT THE LIGHT

SHERIFF Jones had parked in front of his office and was about to get out when he heard the gunshot. His response was neither brave nor sheriffy: he jumped high enough to bang his head on the roof. When he looked around, everybody in sight—including his former schoolteacher Angela Potts—was calmly staring at him.

Red-faced, he glared back. "What *was* that?" he demanded.

Angela, who was sitting on a wooden bench ten feet away, tilted her laptop so he could see the screen. "*Battlestar Command*, version three," she said. "An alien shot at me. I got him, though."

The sudden crackle of static on his police radio was

all that prevented an extremely rude reply. He blew out a sigh and snatched the mike off its hook. "Sheriff Jones here."

It was Sally, his dispatcher. "Where are you?" she said.

"Right outside your office window."

"Call for you."

He heard a click, then a man's gruff voice. "Sheriff? My name's Joe Smith. I got two guys fightin' in my front yard."

Angela, listening, had closed her laptop and was walking toward him.

"Where are you located, Mr. Smith?" the sheriff asked.

"You know the old Varsity Theater? Three-sixteen Oakwood Drive? My house is right across the street."

"Your address?"

"Three-eighteen Oakwood."

"I'm on my way." He had already put the cruiser in gear before he realized Angela had stuffed herself into the passenger seat.

"We," she corrected.

"Look, Ms. Potts—"

"You need me," she said, pointing to her laptop. "I'm a starship commander."

He didn't have the energy to argue. The voice on the radio said, "Turn right at the light, and go straight till you get to—"

"I know where Oakwood Drive is, Mr. Smith. Stay inside, okay?" The sheriff disconnected, drove to the intersection, and headed south.

"Lot of excitement today," Angela said, buckling her seatbelt.

"Jeffy Barrow, you mean?" Young Jeffy had crashed

his pickup into the Civil War statue on the courthouse lawn in the wee hours and was now sleeping it off as a guest of the county. "Don't worry," he said. "My deputies are there, if he wakes up and wonders why he's in a jail cell."

"Your deputies are gone to lunch at Roscoe's."

"Well, Sally's there." The sheriff took his eyes off the road long enough to say, "When we get to this Smith fellow's house, you stay in the car."

Instead of replying, Angela was frowning. She looked preoccupied.

"What?" he said.

"Something sounded fishy, about that address he gave you."

"The address? What do you mean?"

"Matter of fact, on second thought, something else doesn't add up, either." She turned to look at him. "The street in front of your office runs east *and* west. Not just east."

"What are you talking about, Ms. Potts?"

"He said 'turn right at the light.' Which was correct, since we were going east. But he didn't know that, did he. If we'd been headed west, toward the other light, we'd have had to turn left."

The sheriff groaned. "What's your point?"

"My point is, you better turn us around and get back to the station."

"What? *Why?*"

"Because whoever made that call must've been close enough to your office to be watching you," she said. "He saw us leave."

"But—that doesn't make any sense."

"It does if somebody wants to send you on a goosechase

and bust Jeffy Barrow out of jail. And that sounds just like something his crazy daddy would try."

The sheriff considered that. Angela was right—the voice on the phone could indeed have been Harlon Barrow's. He made a tire-screaming U-turn and roared back toward the office and the jail, and sure enough, five minutes later, they caught Harlon and Jeffy Barrow sneaking out of the station house. Behind the escapee and the accomplice, gagged and locked inside Jeffy's cell, was Sally the Dispatcher.

When the Barrows had been reincarcerated and Sally had been freed, the sheriff turned to Angela. "What made you suspicious? His address, you said?"

"That's right," she replied. "It was as phony as everything else."

MYSTERY:

||||||||||||||||||||||||||||||||||||

How did Angela first know something was amiss?

26

BETTER LATE THAN NEVER

Angela Potts was bored.

She shifted in her chair, checked her watch, and wished her friend Janie Mattox would hurry up. It was too nice a day to be indoors.

On the far side of the bank lobby, a dozen customers stood in the teller queue with Janie, waiting far more patiently than Angela was. All were familiar to Angela except for the last two people in line: an elderly lady with a big hat and big purse and a baggy black dress and a young lady with no hat and no purse and a sleeveless, skin-tight red dress. After a moment the older woman turned and Angela realized she knew her after all. That wasn't surprising. Angela knew almost everyone in town.

Finally Angela rose and pushed through the bank's front doors into the sunlight just as someone else she didn't recognize—a short fellow in a flowered shirt—was going in. She plopped down on a bench. The afternoon sun, blazing just above the buildings across the street, felt good.

Four minutes later a strange thing happened: Sheriff Charles Jones screeched a patrol car up to the curb across from the bank. He and Deputy Fred Prewitt jumped out holding shotguns, and crouched behind the car.

"Ms. Potts?" the sheriff shouted. "Get over here."

Angela hurried over and hunkered alongside the two lawmen, behind the cruiser. "What's going on?"

"There's a robbery in progress," the sheriff said, panting. "The alarm sounded at the office."

"I bet I saw the robber," Angela said. "Short guy, yellow shirt—"

At that instant two people emerged from the bank: the man Angela had seen a moment ago, and the customer in the red dress. The man held a pistol in one hand and a moneybag in the other; one arm was clamped around the woman's neck.

The robber saw the patrol car, froze, and for a moment everyone stood there with guns pointed, like a freeze-frame out of a heist movie.

"Hold your fire," the man called out, "or I'll kill her."

And then Angela remembered.

"Chunky," she whispered. "That's not a hostage."

Sheriff Jones, who hadn't been called "Charles" by Angela in thirty years, gave her a hard look. "What?"

The man, still shielded by the woman's body, was

backing slowly toward a car parked nearby.

"The woman's in on it. They're getting away—"

"Not now, Ms. Potts," the sheriff said. Then, loudly: "Let her go, mister."

Angela raised her head to peek over the cruiser's trunk. The man and woman were now halfway to the getaway car. Angela drew a deep breath, reached through the police car's open window, grabbed an electronic bullhorn off the seat, switched it on, ducked out of sight again, and shouted:

"DROP YOUR WEAPON OR WE'LL SHOOT! WE'RE ON THE ROOF ACROSS THE STREET, WE KNOW THE WOMAN'S YOUR ACCOMPLICE, AND WE'LL KILL YOU BOTH!"

Total silence. The sheriff—still pointing his shotgun—gaped at Angela, the deputy gaped at them both, and the two people in front of the bank stopped in their tracks. The man squinted up at the buildings, the sun in his eyes.

"RIGHT *NOW!*" the bullhorn roared.

And three things happened at once: the woman said clearly, "I ain't dying for you, Billy"; she pulled away and raised both hands; and Billy the Bank Robber dropped his pistol.

Sheriff Jones crossed the street and held his gun on the criminals while his deputy handcuffed them both. When Angela arrived he gave her a hard look, but Angela also detected a tiny smile. Then, before being led away, the woman in the red dress asked the sheriff, "Where are the others? The ones with the loudspeaker?"

"Others? Oh. That was my fifth-grade schoolteacher," the sheriff said, nodding to Angela. "She's also the one who knew you weren't really a hostage."

The woman gawked at Angela. "You?"

"I figured it out a little late," Angela said.

"But . . . how? How'd you know?"

"Your pockets," Angela said, pointing at the tight dress.

"What? I don't have any pockets."

Angela smiled. "Exactly."

MYSTERY:
IIIIIIIIIIIIIIIIIIIIIIIIIIIIIIIIIIIIIIIII

Why did Angela suspect that the woman was
in on the robbery?

27

PUPPY LOVE

"**Y**OU took long enough to come pick me up," Angela Potts grumbled.

She and Sheriff Jones were bumping along a dirt road in his patrol car, and her scolding reminded him of the times when she'd taught him in elementary school. He had already decided this would be a bad day, and it was only nine a.m.

"I should've let you walk home," he said. "I'm not the one who had a flat tire."

"You're the one who couldn't fix it."

"You didn't have a spare, Ms. Potts. What am I supposed—"

"Stop the car!" Angela said. She was staring out the

passenger window.

He pulled over in front of Charlotte Cain's house, and as Angela Potts wrenched the door open he saw a blond woman standing beside a roadside tent, squeezing little Timmy Cain's arm and shouting at him.

Angela marched up and asked, "What's going on here?"

"I remember you," the woman said, glaring. "The schoolteacher."

"Retired." Angela was watching the boy, who was red-eyed and sniffling. "Timmy, are you all right?"

"Yes, ma'am."

Angela turned to the woman. "You're Charlotte Cain's sister, right?"

"Yeah." She released the boy's arm. "Lisa Ford, now. I live in Florida."

"Why are you here?"

"I just came to set up shop for a few days—"

"She came to ask my mother for money, Miss Angel," Timmy blurted.

Lisa Ford's face hardened. "Charlotte owes me," she said to Angela, then glanced at the house. "Our daddy left her this place, and I got nothin'."

"If I recall, you're the one who ran off." Angela nodded toward the tent. "What are you selling, here?"

"Handmade jewelry."

"And what's the problem with your nephew?" Sheriff Jones asked.

Ms. Ford's eyes flashed. "He's a thief like his mother. He came down here and sold two puppies that belong to me, and kept the money."

"I did not," Timmy said, sobbing again. "Those were my puppies, and I didn't sell them, I gave 'em to folks who'll give 'em good homes."

"Where's your mother, Timmy?" Angela asked.

"She's in the house there, sick with the flu."

To the woman Angela said, "Why'd you say they were your puppies?"

"Because the mama dog's mine, that's why."

Timmy wailed, "That's not true either. Aunt Lisa didn't want her—Bessie—and gave her to me after my dad died. She didn't even know Bessie'd had puppies until I told her just now."

"When were the puppies born?"

"Last night," he said.

"And you saw Timmy sell them, Ms. Ford?"

Lisa Ford nodded. "I saw him sell 'em right here, this morning, to two different people, and take the cash and run up there to the house with it."

"She's lying," Timmy said. "I told her I gave them away. She never even saw them."

Angela thought a moment, then asked the woman, "What'd they look like?"

"The puppies? They looked like their mother," Ford said. "She's a Dalmatian."

"Be more specific."

"They were white with black spots."

"And who'd you give them to?" Angela asked Timmy.

"I don't know. They were folks who'd stopped to look at Aunt Lisa's stuff."

"See there?" Lisa Ford said. "He sold something that belonged to me, at my place of business. And Dalmatians are expensive."

Angela stared at her awhile, then asked, "Do you have a license to sell merchandise in this state?"

"What?"

"You heard me."

Ford blinked. "Well . . . ah . . ."

Angela looked at the sheriff, who said, "Ms. Ford, I believe you better pack up and go back to Florida."

"But—"

"Or go to jail."

Ford fumed a minute, then growled to Timmy, "You tell your mama I'll be back."

Angela and Sheriff Jones watched Lisa Ford dismantle her tent and load her wares into a truck. After she'd roared away Timmy looked up at them, tears still shining in his eyes, and said, "Thank you."

"My pleasure," Angela said.

"Why'd you believe me and not her?"

Angela smiled. "It was clear as black and white."

MYSTERY:

||||||||||||||||||||||||||||||||||||||||

How did Angela know Lisa Ford was lying?

28

WATCH YOUR STEP

ANGELA Potts entered the sheriff's office as he was polishing off his lunch. He had a drumstick in one hand, a traffic report in the other, and a goofy smile on his face.

"Looks good," she said, dropping into a chair. "KFC?"

"JFC." He held up an empty brown lunchbag. "Jones Fried Chicken. I made it myself. Medium crispy, extra greasy."

"Sounds healthy."

The sheriff nodded and took another bite, leaning over so as not to drip on his paperwork. "I'm a trained professional," he mumbled. "Don't try this at home."

She just sighed. "You heard about Gumbo Harris?"

"No. What about him?"

Before she could reply, the sheriff's intercom buzzed. The metallic voice of his dispatcher said, "A call from Pinewood Apartments, Sheriff. Said Gumbo Harris just fell off a house."

The sheriff wiped his mouth with a napkin and reached for his hat. "How do you always know things so fast, Ms. Potts?"

"My informants are many," she said. "How about a ride?"

Minutes later they pulled up outside the Pinewood complex's office. Its developer, Gary Loomis, strolled out to greet them. It was a hot day, with not a breath of wind. Both of them studied Loomis, who looked like a regular guy but was rumored to be knee-deep in loan-sharking and gambling.

"What happened?" the sheriff asked him.

"An accident, Sheriff. Terrible thing. Come over here with me, I'll show you."

He and Angela followed Loomis up the stairs of an apartment building under construction. On the fourth floor Loomis pointed to a closed door at the end of a hallway. "See that door? My foreman—Gumbo's cousin Bud—was showing Gumbo around when he wandered away and walked out that door."

"What's on the other side?" Angela asked.

To answer the question, Loomis led them back down-stairs and around the building, where he stopped and pointed again. The closed door they'd just seen was for-ty feet up the side of the structure, set in a blank wall. There was nothing but thin air on this side.

"What's this?" the sheriff asked.

"What's it look like? It's an unfinished floor on an unfinished building. That idiot Gumbo just opened the door and stepped out into space." Loomis stared at the hardpacked ground below it. "He landed right there. They hauled his body away twenty minutes ago."

"Anybody been up there since?"

"No. Nobody's been anywhere near the door, or that end of the floor. A tragic accident, Sheriff."

Angela and the sheriff exchanged a look. After a long moment he nodded his understanding and turned again to Loomis. "I hear Gumbo Harris owed you money," the sheriff said.

Loomis said sadly, "That's right."

"How much?"

He shrugged. "Several thousand. Guess now I'll never collect it."

"How long's he been in your debt?"

"A while. Gumbo had some bad habits, you know?"

"What about you, Gary?" Angela asked. "You have any bad habits?"

Loomis did a palms-up. "Hey, I'm innocent here, okay? That fool did it to himself. What, you think I'd kill somebody owed me that much money?"

"I hear a lot of people owe you money," the sheriff said. "I hear sometimes you feel you have to make an example of those who don't pay up."

Loomis shook his head. "You got me all wrong, Sheriff."

"We'll see. Meanwhile, you're under arrest for murder."

"What?! You think—"

"I think you walked Mr. Harris to the end of that hall, opened the door, and pushed him out. That's what I think."

"And how you gonna prove that?"

"An eyewitness," Sheriff Jones said. "Looking out her window, from across the street over there. Says she saw the whole thing."

That got Loomis's attention. The bravado melted away. "Wait a minute—I ain't pushed *no*body."

"Who did?"

Loomis swallowed. "My foreman. Bud Wilson."

"On whose orders, I wonder," the sheriff said.

Afterward, when Loomis and Wilson had been handcuffed and loaded into the squad car, Angela looked at the sheriff and said, "What eyewitness?"

He grinned. "My informants are *not* many," he said. "Sometimes I make them up."

MYSTERY:

What was the clue that told him Gumbo Harris had been murdered?

29

HOMELAND SECURITY

"THANKS for letting me hitch a ride," Angela Potts said. She and Deputy Fred Prewitt were dining at a table in a hotel in the state capital. Angela had attended a gardening conference all day and Prewitt had been competing in the regional police marksmanship finals. She'd learned how to fertilize tomato plants and he'd placed third in the pistol category. They were headed home tomorrow.

The Homeland Hotel had been a pleasant surprise. Antique desks, free DVD library, chocolates on the pillow, card-activated room entry, bathroom telephones— even this private dining area for "guests only."

"Glad you came along," he replied. "And thanks for

meeting me for supper."

Angela was about to respond when she noticed something several tables away. A man sitting alone had dropped his napkin and stooped to retrieve it.

Prewitt saw her frown. "What is it?"

She said, keeping her eyes on the man, "Don't look now. You remember seeing two middle-aged ladies at a table over there, when we came in?"

"I think so. Why?"

"They're still there, and a guy is by himself at the table next to them. He's sitting back-to-back to one of the ladies."

"So?"

"Her purse is hanging from her chair back. I think he just bent over and stole something from it."

Prewitt risked a quick glance. "What'd he steal?"

"Don't know," she said. "See him? Blue suit, dark hair."

"I see him."

"You still have your gun under your jacket?"

"Yes—I just got in from the range."

"Got your badge?"

"In my pocket. Why?"

"You have to arrest him," she said.

"What?" Prewitt stared at her. "I can't arrest him, Ms. Potts. We're out of our jurisdiction."

"Jurisdiction my butt. The man's a thief."

"You're sure of that?"

"Well, no," she admitted. "But I think so."

"What if you're wrong?"

"Ask Sheriff Jones, sometime, if I'm usually wrong."

Prewitt frowned, thinking hard. "What do you think the sheriff would do, in this situation?"

Angela sighed. "He'd finish his supper, belch, and never give it another thought."

"Exactly."

"But we can't do that, Fred."

Prewitt turned a bit in his chair, held up the dessert menu, and studied the "suspect" from the corner of his eye. As they watched, the man took a large gold key from his pocket, looked at it, repocketed it, and signed something lying on the table.

"He's about to leave, Ms. Potts," Prewitt said. "He just charged his meal to his room number."

"No he didn't," Angela said. "He just wanted us to think he did."

"What?"

Before she could reply, the man rose from his table, left the dining area, and disappeared into a men's room visible just outside the doorway.

Angela had had enough. She signaled the waiter, told him to call hotel security, marched out, and stood in front of the restroom door. Waiting.

Prewitt hurried after her. "Wait a second, Ms. Potts, we can't confront him. We have no evidence."

"You're right. *He* has the evidence."

"What if we ask the lady if she's missing anything?"

"There's no time, Fred. I know what I saw. And I'm sure now."

"Sure of what?"

"That he's guilty."

"But how—"

At that point the man stepped out of the restroom.

"My friend here is a deputy sheriff," Angela informed him. "You're under arrest."

The man blinked. "For what?"

"Robbery, that's what. Would you kindly turn out your pockets?"

He hesitated a moment, then emptied his pockets into Angela's outstretched hand. Car keys, wallet, breath-mints, gold-plated room key, penknife, loose change. Angela flipped through the wallet's contents: credit cards, driver's license, several twenties. Nothing else.

"Fred," she said, "check the restroom."

"Ms. Potts—"

"Check it." She held her breath until Prewitt re-appeared a minute later, holding a shiny black smart-phone.

"Found it behind a toilet tank," Prewitt said. "He must've seen us watching him and stowed it there."

At that moment a security guy arrived. He listened to their story, verified that the phone belonged to one of the two ladies, and led the scowling thief away.

Prewitt looked wonderingly at Angela, who looked back at him and winked.

MYSTERY:
||||||||||||||||||||||||||||||||||||||

What had convinced Angela that the man was guilty?

30

NO TRESPASSING

SHERIFF Chunky Jones was annoyed to see Angela Potts's gas guzzler parked at Mabel Wallace's house when he arrived—but he wasn't surprised. Ms. Potts, who had taught him in grade school, could find trouble as easily as his golf balls could find water.

She and businessman Pete Peterson were standing on the front porch with Ms. Wallace, who had called in to report that she'd seen a prowler last night. All three were huddled into heavy coats. December in the Deep South was seldom warm, but this year it was frigid.

"I saw him outside my living room window, Sheriff," Ms. Wallace said. "Around nine o'clock. I screamed, and as he ran off I spotted a Peterson's Sporting Goods logo on his jacket. Pete here says he has only three guys who weren't on duty last night."

"Why'd you wait till today to report it?"

"An icy limb broke my phone line yesterday. They fixed it this morning."

"I brought the three boys over, Sheriff," Peterson said. "They're waiting inside."

The sheriff shot a worried look at Angela.

"Don't worry," she told him, grinning. "I haven't questioned them yet."

He harrumphed. "I always worry."

"You can say that again."

"I always worry," he said.

The suspects were all in their late teens. The first, Jason Burns, told the sheriff and Angela that he'd been out with his girlfriend until midnight, and that she could verify it. The second, Jim Santos, claimed he'd been on a long-distance call to his mother at the time. He'd been concerned since she was snowed in—she'd said the winter there was even worse than the one here. The third employee, Donald Chang, was home alone last night, but was wearing an alibi—a bandage on his ankle that would have kept him from running.

"This girlfriend of yours," the sheriff said to Burns. "Where is she now?"

"Christmas shopping. I called her a minute ago."

Mabel Wallace snorted. "And told her to back up his story, probably."

The sheriff turned to Santos. "Where's your mother live, son?"

"Argentina," Santos said.

"Did you use a home phone or a cell?"

"My house."

"And you, Chang. When and how'd you hurt your leg?"

"Slipped on the ice yesterday afternoon," the boy answered. "On my back steps."

"Sure it wasn't while running home from here?" Ms. Wallace snapped.

The sheriff studied their work jackets. "Do you guys wear those when you're not on duty?"

"Sure," Burns said. "They're warm."

The four older folks excused themselves. Once outside, the sheriff sighed, his breath making a cloud in the freezing air. "Ms. Wallace, a trespassing charge isn't serious enough to detain them. We can check phone records and the injury and so forth, but it'll take awhile. Or—"

"No waiting," Mabel Wallace said. "They might leave town."

"—or I can give them a warning and we'll let it go."

She blinked. "A warning? Are you kidding? Someone was lurking around my house last night!"

"At your window? On your porch? Or just in your yard?"

"My yard. Does it matter?"

Another sigh. "Ms. Wallace, these boys all live nearby—one was probably cutting across your lawn so he wouldn't have to walk a quarter mile to the main road. I used to do that myself."

"Then why doesn't whoever did it just say that?"

"Because all three of them are scared to death, that's why."

"They're pretty good boys, Mabel," Pete Peterson said.

Ms. Wallace fumed a minute, then nodded. Afterward, as the sheriff and Angela crunched through the frozen slush to their cars, she said, "Good work, Chunky. I'm proud of you."

He shrugged. "Mostly, I hated to take the time to check it all out, for something like this. Mabel Wallace has always been hotheaded."

"Well, I agree. I'd hate to see him go to jail for taking a shortcut."

"Him?" The sheriff squinted at her. "You know which one did it?"

She smiled. "I know which one wasn't telling the truth."

MYSTERY:
||||||||||||||||||||||||||||||||||

Which of the three young men was lying?

31

THE FAMILY JEWELS

SHERIFF Jones was in a bad mood. He was hungry (his wife had him on a diet), he was sleepy (his head had hurt all night), and the bossy lady sitting in his office had been bossing him around ever since he was her fifth-grade student. Besides all that—

"The paper didn't even mention that I was injured at the scene," he said, jabbing a finger at an inside-page headline: EMBEZZLER CAPTURED AT REMOTE CAMPSITE.

"As I recall," Angela Potts said, "you bashed your head into a tree while running *away* from the scene."

"I was going for reinforcements. The suspect was waving a gun around."

"A toy gun," she said. "In fact, a water pistol."

"How was *I* supposed to know that?"

Angela sighed. "Admit it—you're just mad because I'm the one who figured out where he was hiding."

The sheriff, still sulking, said, "How do you *do* that? Can you think like a criminal?"

"No, I just watch for inconsistencies. Things that don't make sense."

"Why can't I do that?"

"You can." She added, in her schoolteacher voice, "All liars aren't lawbreakers, but most lawbreakers are liars. You have to listen for things that don't add up."

Before he could reply, his desk phone rang. It made his head start hurting again. He pointed at the phone and said, "Sally's on her break. Make yourself useful."

Angela picked up the receiver. "Sheriff's office." She listened a moment, said, "It's Fred Prewitt," and pressed the speaker button.

"I'm at Fowler Jewelers," Deputy Prewitt said. "Armed robbery, just before I drove by. Suspect got away with a fortune in diamond necklaces. Only one person was manning the store."

"Orville Fowler?" Angela asked.

"His son Danny. He moved here recently with his wife. Orville's home sick."

"Description of the suspect?" the sheriff said.

"Danny said it was a white male, fortyish, dark hair, blue shirt and jacket, tan pants. Belt had a gold 'J' on the buckle."

"No other witnesses?"

"Just one lady on the street, who saw Danny Fowler walking back to the store from his car, afterward."

"His car?"

"According to Danny," Prewitt said, "he ran outside to give chase, got into his Toyota, and then realized pursuit was useless—the suspect was already gone. Getaway car was a black Ford Escort."

The sheriff was taking notes. "Anything else?"

He and Angela heard an exchange of words, then Prewitt came back on the speaker and said, "Danny says the thief was also wearing running shoes, and red suspenders."

Angela asked, "How'd he see suspenders underneath a jacket?"

"Says the guy pulled back the coat to draw his gun."

"What kind?" the sheriff asked.

"Short-barreled revolver."

"Have you spoken to the other witness?"

"Yep. The lady outside saw only Danny, getting out of his car. She never saw the robber or the getaway vehicle."

The sheriff was frowning, deep in thought. He and Angela exchanged a look. Into the speaker he said, "I don't think there *was* a getaway vehicle, Fred. Or a robber, for that matter."

"Excuse me?"

"I think the 'stolen' jewels are in Danny Fowler's Toyota."

"What?!"

"Ask him if you can search his car."

Prewitt lowered his voice. "Wouldn't I need a search warrant?"

The sheriff glanced at Angela, who was smiling, and said, "Only if you search it. You don't need one to *ask* him."

Again, they heard an exchange of voices. Then

something else—sounds of a scuffle, and shouts. Several minutes later Prewitt came back on. He sounded out of breath.

"Sheriff? You there?"

"We're here. What happened?"

"When I asked Fowler if I could search his car, he went pale as a ghost, then took off for the door. I caught him, and he started babbling that his wife made him steal the jewelry. Said she wanted a bigger house."

"Well, he'll be in one, shortly. Bring him in, Fred."

The sheriff hung up and looked at Angela, who was still grinning.

"I couldn't have done better myself," she said. "What tipped you off?"

"An inconsistency," he said.

MYSTERY:

*What made Sheriff Jones suspect that
Danny Fowler was lying?*

32

HEAT WAVE

"How hot's it supposed to get, today?" Angela asked.

"Weatherman said 101."

"I think it's already there." Angela Potts and her friend Betty Fenwick were eating lunch on a shaded park bench, and only the stiff breeze made it bearable. Nearby, a riding mower roared its way across a scorched lawn surrounding a public pool. The asphalt parking lot beside the bench was hot enough to fry an egg on its surface.

Betty said, "I remember one August—"

A shout startled them both: "Help! I've been robbed!"

Angela turned to see, in the distance, old Gus Simpson in his concession booth at the edge of the parking lot, and an unfamiliar woman standing near him. It was Gus who'd shouted, but the woman looked as alarmed as he was. Angela rose, told Betty to stay put, and hurried toward them through the shimmering heat.

When she got there, puffing, Angela said, "What is it, Gus? Who robbed you?"

Gus Simpson wore dark glasses—he'd been blind from birth. "Don't know," he stammered. "I heard a lady giving somebody directions, then felt my cashbox snatched out of my lap. My cashbox!"

"Where's your wife?"

"I forgot my medicine—she went home to get it for me." The Simpsons had tended a snack stand here for many years, selling burgers and hotdogs. Angela saw a tear run down his cheek.

She turned to the lady, who still looked flustered. "Who are you?"

"Janice Burke. I'm visiting, from Florida." She held up a green beach-bag. "I was walking across the parking lot here, headed down to the pool to cool off, when all this happened."

"Tell me what you saw."

Ms. Burke swallowed. "A little kid—maybe ten years old—asked me where he could buy a stamp for a letter. I told him how to get to the post office, turned my back, and before I knew it he grabbed this man's money and ran off."

"Which way?"

Burke pointed across the lot. Angela thought for a moment, then waved to the workman mowing the grass. He dismounted and strolled over to stand beside them on the pavement. When Angela asked if he'd seen a running child, he shook his head.

"Gus," she said to Simpson, "what did you hear?"

"Just this lady's voice, talking to someone."

"You hear the other voice too?"

"Nope, just her. Then my money got stole, I hollered blue murder, and I heard you jogging over here."

"You didn't hear the thief run off?"

"No—"

"He wouldn't have," Ms. Burke said. "The kid was barefooted. Besides, that lawnmower was really loud."

Angela studied her closely. "If the robber was a kid, why didn't you chase him?"

"Because I was barefoot too. I had to dig my shoes out of my bag here, and then put them on."

Angela kept looking at her. Finally she lowered her gaze to the woman's beach bag. "Nice color," Angela said. She touched the bag but snagged its strap in the process—"Oops!"—and it fell to the ground. With a loud CLANK.

Everyone froze.

"How clumsy of me," Angela said. She stooped and saw, inside the bag, the corner of a metal cashbox.

She pointed at the workman. "You," she said. "Grab this lady's arm and hold her. Gus, find your cell phone and call the sheriff."

Ms. Burke's face sagged. She seemed to realize struggling was useless. As they waited for the Law to arrive, Angela said to the woman, "You made the kid up, didn't you. And you didn't figure on Gus shouting so loud and attracting so much attention before you could get away."

Janice Burke nodded miserably. Then she said, "You spilled my bag on purpose, didn't you."

"Sorry about that."

Burke closed her eyes and sighed. "I thought

pretending to speak to a kid would be a good cover, if something went wrong."

"It might have, if not for the directions. It seemed strange that you, a visitor, would know where our post office was," Angela said. "But even that didn't convince me you were lying."

"What did?"

Angela smiled. "The weather."

MYSTERY:

|||||||||||||||||||||||||||||||||||||||

What made Angela doubt the woman's story?

33

NUMBER, PLEASE

SHERIFF Charles Jones was exhausted, and for good reason. He and his former schoolteacher, Angela Potts, had been trudging through the moonlit countryside for hours.

"The one person on earth," he grumbled, "who doesn't carry a cell phone."

"It's at home," she said. "At least I didn't drop mine into a cup full of coffee."

He could feel his blood pressure rising. "It's *my* car, Ms. Potts, and *my* cup-holder's always empty. That's where I keep my phone. How was I to know you'd put your coffee cup in there?"

"Because that's what cup-holders are for," she said.

The sheriff huffed out a sigh. First his cruiser had broken down, and now this. "Any idea where we are?"

"Zack and Ned French's land, I think. We should've kept to the main road."

"I thought this was a short cut."

Suddenly Angela squinted, and pointed west. "House lights. Maybe a mile away."

"Forget it. Town's in the other direction."

"I bet that's the French house. They could give us a ride."

"How you gonna call 'em?" he asked—

And tripped over the body.

"Jeez Louise!" he shouted. Lying there at their feet in the middle of nowhere was a dead man in jeans and a windbreaker. "What in the—"

Angela was staring at the face. "It's Max Ross. Investigative reporter, from Memphis. I saw him when he was interviewed last month on TV."

"What's he doing down here?"

"Maybe the same thing we were," she said. Two men had fled in this direction last week after robbing First Exchange Bank, and the sheriff and Angela had been questioning rural residents. At least until his phone drowned and his patrol car died.

The sheriff gazed at the distant lights. "Maybe he was spying on the Frenches."

"For the bank robbery, you mean?

"It's possible, right? They live on the escape route."

Still shaken, they both studied the body. The moon went behind a cloud, and Angela switched on a flashlight. "You think the French Brothers could've killed him?"

"Whoever did, did it here. He wasn't transported

afterward. Look at all the blood."

"Should we search him?"

"No. But . . ." The sheriff looked closer. A corner of a note jutted from his shirt pocket. Angela retrieved it and held it by one corner in the flashlight's beam. Printed on the paper were the letters FXHEIST.

"What's this?" he asked.

Angela frowned. "The robbery, I guess. 'First Exchange heist.'"

"But why's it written down? What does it mean?"

"Beats me. But I know Max Ross was a puzzle fanatic. And secretive."

"So?"

"So this could be a coded message."

"For who?"

"For whom," she corrected. "Maybe for us."

"Us?"

"The good guys. Maybe he suspected danger, and didn't want the bad guys—if worse came to worst—to discover he was onto something."

"Looks like they did anyway." Then the sheriff noticed a rectangular bulge in Ross's jeans pocket. "Whoa—is that a cell phone?"

He carefully removed it, and called in to report their discovery of the body. He also asked dispatch for the phone number of the Frenches' home. To Angela he said, "Write this down: three-nine-four-three-four-seven-eight. In case we need it."

"I agree," she replied—and froze.

"What's wrong?" he asked.

She aimed the flashlight at her notepad. "Call it a French connection."

"What?"

143

Angela looked up. "Witnesses described the getaway car as an old white pickup, right?"

"Yes."

"Well, Zack French was in town yesterday in an old green pickup. I thought nothing of it then—but maybe you should have Deputy Prewitt get a search warrant and check Zack's truck for a white undercoat."

"Why? What did you see that's so interesting?"

After she'd explained, Sheriff Jones phoned his deputy. An hour later, Angela and Prewitt and the sheriff found, in the Frenches' barn, not only a newly-painted truck but two dozen bank bags and a Tennessee car registered to a Maxwell Ross. Both brothers were arrested on the spot.

"Poor Max," Angela said. "He would've made a good detective."

MYSTERY:

What had Angela noticed that pointed her toward Zack and Ned French?

34

THE LISTENER

SHERIFF Charles Jones stomped into his office and announced, "Don't ever let anybody tell you a root canal's painless—"

And stopped. Three people were sitting there: his former teacher Angela Potts, Deputy Fred Prewitt, and a young man he didn't know.

Prewitt motioned the sheriff outside. "While you were at the dentist's," he said quietly, "dispatch got a call from a woman on Webster Street, said she'd seen a man in a white T-shirt and blue jeans sneaking out of the house owned by her neighbor, a George Sullivan. I was on patrol near there, and since she said the guy had headed east into Heritage Park, I drove around and caught this dude coming out the east side of the park. Name's Jack Nelson."

"Have you arrested him?"

"We're not positive it's the same guy," Prewitt replied. "The neighbor only saw his clothes."

"Why's Ms. Potts here?"

"Isn't she usually here?"

The sheriff rolled his eyes. "True enough. But why's she sitting in the office with the suspect?"

"She arrived when we did, and I agreed to let her sit in on the questioning." Prewitt squinted at the sheriff a minute. "How's the tooth?"

"Don't ask." They re-entered the office, where the sheriff pulled up a chair and faced the suspect. "Let's hear your story," he said.

Jack Nelson took a long breath. "I'm innocent, Sheriff. I'd never heard of this Mr. Sullivan before, and I'd never been to his house. Some neighbor lady says I was there today, but I wasn't."

"Anything stolen?" the sheriff asked Prewitt.

"Cash and jewelry. Sullivan found it all missing when he got back from a trip to the supermarket."

"Anything in your pockets, Mr. Nelson?"

"No sir. Your deputy's already searched me."

"What were you doing in the park?"

"Nothing. I'm sort of a handyman, and I'm between jobs."

"A Jack of all trades?"

"Very funny," Nelson said glumly.

The sheriff looked at Angela. She hadn't said a word since he arrived; she was just staring at the suspect. Jack Nelson took that opportunity to point to her and ask, "What's she doing here, anyway?"

"I'm a consultant," Angela answered, with a straight face. "Mostly, I just listen."

"Listen for what?"

"Listen to see if you say something wrong."

That stopped him for a moment, and during the pause the sheriff said, "Continue, Mr. Nelson. You were telling me what happened."

"Well . . . your deputy here walked up and said to get in the car with him. He told me about the burglary and took me back to the house. This Sullivan guy looked me over and said he hadn't seen me before—which was true."

"Only because he wasn't home at the time."

"No, because you got the wrong *man*, Sheriff."

"What about the description?"

"Come on—you think I'm the only guy in town who's wearing a white T-shirt and jeans?"

"You might be the only one wearing them in the park today."

Jack Nelson spread his hands. "How do you think I got rid of the stolen goods? Hid them someplace?"

Angela stood up, approached the sheriff, and whispered something in his ear.

He turned to Nelson, paused a moment, and said, "I think that's exactly what you did. I think we'll find it, too—but I have a proposition: tell us where it is and things'll go easier for you."

"So you *do* think I'm guilty?"

"I know you are. You're under arrest, by the way. Fred, read him his rights and lock him up."

Nelson's eyes bugged out. "What? Wait—wait a minute here."

"Yes?"

He sighed, and swallowed. "Okay. Okay, I was broke, all right? I saw a house with an open window and an empty garage. Afterward, I realized the neighbor might've seen me so I figured I better stash the loot. I stuffed it into a storm drain in the park."

Prewitt took him by the arm to lead him away while the sheriff and Angela exchanged a satisfied look. Nelson caught the look and asked her bitterly, "How did you know?"

Angela smiled. "Because you said something wrong."

MYSTERY:
||||||||||||||||||||||||||||||||||||||||

What did Angela hear that convinced her
Jack Nelson was guilty?

35

BUS STOP

SHERIFF Charles Taylor Jones was leaning against his cruiser with the hood up and his cell phone pressed to his ear when his former teacher Angela Potts rumbled up beside him in her seen-better-days Buick.

"Hey, sailor," she said. "Looking for a good time?"

"I wouldn't know a good time if I saw it."

"Need a ride, then?"

"What I need's a new patrol car," he said, looking glum. "And stop grinning."

He pocketed his phone, climbed into the passenger seat, and pointed east. "There's a reported schoolbus accident on Greenfield Road, plus a tornado sighting. If you could drop me off—"

"Buckle your lapstrap," she said.

Five nerve-jangling minutes later they stood and watched the body of Lester McWilliams being loaded into an ambulance. A scruffy dog lounged near the sheriff's feet. The empty schoolbus Lester had been driving was sitting on the road's grassy shoulder, its front bumper resting against a tree trunk. Faraway thunder rumbled, and dark stormclouds receded in the distance.

"Thank goodness he had already taken all the kids home," Norman Kimbrough said to them.

Kimbrough, a bank manager, said he'd been driving along and watching the threatening weather when he saw the schoolbus ease off the road with Lester slumped unconscious over its steering wheel. The bus had coasted into a sweetgum tree just as a funnel dipped from the churning clouds nearby. According to Kimbrough, he had jumped out of his car, boarded the bus through the front side door, and dragged the inert Lester out to the safety of a drainage ditch. Then he dashed back in to rescue Lester's dog, which was cowering in fear of the howling winds.

The storm stayed aloft and spared them, Kimbrough said—but Lester never regained consciousness. Since Lester was known to have a weak heart, Kimbrough suspected he might have already expired before the bus even left the road.

When he'd finished his story, Norman Kimbrough asked to be excused. He was campaigning for mayor, he reminded them, and said he was late for a newspaper interview downtown.

"I can see the headline now," Angela said, after he'd left. "LOCAL BANKER RISKS LIFE IN DARING RESCUE."

Sheriff Jones shrugged. "I suppose he *is* a hero, even if Lester had already passed. It took courage to do what Kimbrough did."

"If he did what he *says* he did," Angela corrected.

"What do you mean?"

"Kimbrough told us he unbuckled Lester from the driver's seat and dragged him to safety, then went back in and carried the dog out too, right?"

"So?"

She pointed to the muddy tracks leading from the bus to the ditch. "There's only one set of human footprints here, and they're huge. Lester was a really big guy—Kimbrough's not. And right beside the footprints are the tracks of a dog. A dog walking on the ground, not being carried."

The sheriff frowned. "You're saying you think Lester and his dog got out of the bus on their own?"

"I'm saying Lester probably never lost consciousness on the bus, and that Kimbrough never went to the bus at all. I bet Lester staggered out and took cover in the ditch and then died there, with or without Norm Kimbrough beside him."

The sheriff sighed. "What difference does it make? This isn't a police matter. No crime was committed here, except maybe Lester allowing his pet to ride on the bus."

Angela snorted. "You want to see a crime? Norman Kimbrough getting elected mayor would be a crime. He's a fake and a liar, Chunky. You know that."

"What I know is, there was only one eyewitness, and to dispute that eyewitness I'm going to need more evidence than muddy footprints. Maybe Kimbrough was *carrying* Lester instead of dragging him—the extra weight might make the tracks look bigger. And maybe the dog walked part of the way on his own, once Kimbrough hauled him out."

She shook her head. "It's not just the tracks. There's no way things could've happened the way Kimbrough said they did."

"How do you know?"

"Because I've driven schoolbuses before," Angela said.

MYSTERY:

Why was Angela certain that Norm Kimbrough's heroic story was false?

36

PICTURE THIS

ANGELA Potts noticed, as she plopped down on the park bench beside Sheriff Jones, that he looked grumpy—but that was nothing unusual.

"What are you doing here, Ms. Potts?"

"Trying to cheer you up." She took a digital camera from her purse, aimed it, and snapped his picture.

"Well, it's not working," he growled. Then: "Is that a new camera?"

"I bought it so I could take pictures at the Thursday Bingo game, at the church. I'm the new editor of the newsletter." She held up the camera and showed him photos of the Bingo crowd. "That was three days ago, before I learned to use the zoom—but not bad, huh?"

"I guess. Why'd you take a picture of *me*?"

"Rabbits have been eating my tomato plants," she said. "Figured if I put your photo up in my garden—"

"Very funny," he said.

Smiling, Angela turned and took a few pictures of the backs of the buildings lining one side of the town square. Their bench was at the edge of a city park one street south of the square; the sheriff's car was parked nearby, in the shade of a live oak.

"If you have to feel sorry for yourself," she said, "at least feel happy for *me*—this photography thing's been a lot of fun. Want to see my pictures of Henrietta and Beulah Puckett?"

"I'll pass." He stayed quiet a moment, frowning, and added, "If you really want to scare off your rabbits, use Henrietta's picture. That should do the job."

She eyed him closely. "Boy, you *are* in a bad mood, aren't you. And you look dead tired."

The sheriff was gazing off into the distance. "Just depressed. I mean, all I do is write parking tickets, Ms. Potts. When something interesting happens, something serious, *you* always solve the case."

"Not always," she said. She held the camera up and showed him another photo. "Look how sharp this is. Beulah looks pretty good, for eighty."

The sheriff sighed and rubbed his face. "I need a vacation," he mumbled.

Angela glanced up from her camera to see a young blond man strolling along behind the downtown buildings. She snapped his picture as he climbed into a small blue car parked at the curb.

"Or maybe I just need to retire," he said. "I could hunt and fish anytime I feel like it, and—"

"Did you see that guy?" she asked.

"What?"

"That guy." She pointed at the car, which had pulled out and was headed west, toward the interstate. "Hot as it is today, he was wearing an overcoat. A baggy overcoat."

"Oh. Yeah, I saw him. He came out the door of the bank."

Angela blinked. "The back entrance?"

The sheriff gave her a weary look. "We're facing the back sides of the buildings, Ms. Potts. We can't *see* the front entrance."

She fell silent a moment, thinking. "I passed Deputy Prewitt's cruiser awhile ago, parked beside the highway west of here. Is he still there?"

"Probably. We've had a lot of complaints lately, about speeders on that stretch of—"

"Call him," she said. "Quick. Tell him to stop that car we just saw. Blue Toyota, Kentucky plates, tag number"—she looked down at her camera, found the image—"R T B four one nine."

"Why should I do that?"

"You *must* be tired. You don't find anything unusual about what that guy just did?"

"No," he said. "Why?"

Suddenly he remembered. And understood. "He must've robbed the bank!"

"My thoughts exactly," she said. "Call Prewitt."

The sheriff grabbed his cell phone and made the call. But when he disconnected and calmed down, he was scowling again.

"What's the matter?" Angela asked. "If this guy really robbed First National and Prewitt catches him—you're a hero."

"Not me. You are. I overlooked the completely obvious. You figured it out."

She smiled and shook her head. "*You* figured it out," she said. "I'm just a photographer."

MYSTERY:

Why had Angela suspected that the man they'd seen had robbed the bank?

37

BREAKING NEWS

Retired schoolteacher Angela Potts found Sheriff Charles Jones stretched out on a park bench, his head on one armrest and his boots on the other.

"It's ninety degrees out here," she said, staring down at him. "How can you possibly be asleep?"

He sat up and rubbed his eyes with his knuckles. "Years of practice. What do you want, Ms. Potts?"

"It's your deputy who wants you—he's been looking everywhere. Where's your cell phone?"

"In my car."

"Where's your car?"

"Over there," he said, pointing. "Why?"

She grabbed his arm and marched him in that

direction. "We're needed at Trudy Martin's place. She says her wedding ring was stolen."

"But Trudy Martin's divorced."

"You'd make a great detective, Chunky."

"What?"

"Just because her husband's gone, doesn't mean her ring's gone too." Angela said. Then she frowned and added, "Well, I guess the ring *is* gone too, now. Anyhow, we got a burglar to catch."

They wedged themselves into the sheriff's cruiser and headed west. "What happened, exactly?" he asked her.

"Trudy says somebody came through the window of her baby son's bedroom sometime last night and stole her ring off her dresser. Never even woke the baby. She discovered the loss this morning."

"Anything else?"

"That's all Prewitt told me," Angela said.

They arrived at the Martins' home to find Trudy and her little one sitting in chairs in the yard. Deputy Fred Prewitt showed the sheriff and Angela the apparent point of entry. They checked everything out, but saw nothing unusual except pieces of broken window-glass on the floor of the baby's room.

When they returned to the yard to interview Trudy, they found her calm and composed. Her nine-month-old son, perched on her lap, grinned at them both.

"How long you think it'll be before they let me collect the insurance?" Trudy asked the sheriff.

"On the ring? I wouldn't know, Ms. Martin. Have you reported it already? Filed a claim?"

"You bet I did."

"Well, I need to ask you some questions," he said. "You told Deputy Prewitt the burglar took your ring from your bedroom dresser, right?"

"No, no—I'm a light sleeper, I would've heard him if he came into my room. The ring was in a drawer in the guest room."

The sheriff frowned, thinking. "And nothing else is missing?"

"Not that I know of."

"How could he have known where you kept the ring?"

"Beats me."

Angela leaned forward and said, "Ms. Martin, something's bothering me. You said the burglar didn't wake your baby?"

"That's right."

"How do you know?"

"Excuse me?"

"The baby's room's over on the other side of the house. How do you know your son didn't wake up and then go back to sleep?"

"Because he didn't cry," Trudy said. "I have a baby monitor, see, and it's always turned on so I can hear little Davey if he needs me—and last night I never even heard a peep out of him."

The sheriff sighed, stood up, and put his notepad away. "Well, thanks for your time, Ms. Martin."

As they were headed for the door, Angela said to the sheriff, loud enough that Trudy could hear, "This reminds me of what happened to Daisy Flowers, awhile back. Remember that?"

"Daisy Flowers?" he said.

"You know, the lady who claimed her Chinese vase was stolen." With a raised eyebrow Angela said to Trudy, "Turned out she'd hidden it, and just wanted to collect the insurance. Not that you'd do that, of course."

Trudy swallowed. "What happened to her? Ms. Flowers, I mean."

"Oh, she's fine. She'll be up for parole in about two more years." Angela turned to leave. "Thanks again, Ms. Martin."

They made it halfway to the car before Trudy Martin called to them.

"Sheriff," she said, "I, ah, I think I just remembered where my ring might be . . ."

• • •

Afterward, on the way back downtown, the sheriff said to Angela, "Funny thing, Ms. Potts: I've lived here my whole life—and I never once heard the name 'Daisy Flowers.'"

Angela just smiled. "It's a pretty name, though. Isn't it."

MYSTERY:

What made Angela think Trudy Martin was lying?

38

GAME PLAN

WHEN Sheriff Charles Jones arrived at the Daley residence, he found investigator Angela Potts waiting for him. The problem was, he said to himself, Angela only *thought* she was an investigator. Her actual credentials were: (1) retired schoolteacher, (2) puzzle addict, and (3) Pain in the Sheriff's Backside.

"Why are you here, Ms. Potts?" he asked wearily.

She snorted. "Why do you think? I'm here to help you solve a murder."

"What's to solve?" He pointed to the house. "Ms. Daley's husband's dead, and she told my deputy she saw Lewis Larrimore kill him."

"She didn't *see* anything. She says she was outside

161

when it happened."

"Don't tell me—you questioned her?"

"Along with your deputy," she said. "Who was at least here on time."

The sheriff sighed and pushed past her into the house. They found Deputy Fred Prewitt in the den with a tearful Susan Daley and a lady neighbor. Susan looked like the outdoor type: flannel shirt, shorts, white socks, hiking boots.

Between sobs, Susan repeated her story. Her ex-husband Buster, released from prison this morning, had asked last week to stay here with her for a few days. She reluctantly agreed, and gave him her spare room. While Buster was napping this afternoon, his friend Lewis Larrimore had stopped by. He was in the room with Buster only a few minutes, Susan said, then left. When she checked a moment later she found Buster lying dead in his bed. Deputy Prewitt responded to her 911 call, and soon confirmed the cause of death: a blow to the right temple from a blunt instrument.

The sheriff turned to the neighbor, Jill Bickham. "You came over just after Ms. Daley discovered the body?"

Bickham nodded. "I always come around three o'clock, for coffee. I saw a light in the spare bedroom, and when Susan didn't answer my call I went in. Everything was spilled, and she was standing there staring at Buster."

"Spilled?" Angela asked.

"Take a look," Prewitt said. They walked to the bedroom, where the body had been removed but the floor was littered with an overturned cardtable, a Chinese checkers board, and dozens of half-inch gray steel balls.

"We'd lost the set of marbles," Susan explained, "so we used ball-bearings as playing pieces. Since Buster loved board games, I fetched this one and we played to-day after lunch. I guess Lew accidentally knocked over the table when he left." She paused and added, "When he *fled*."

"So you're absolutely convinced that Lewis Larrimore killed your husband?" the sheriff said.

"Ex," Susan corrected. "And who else could've done it? There's no murder weapon here—Jill can tell you that. Lewis hit him with something big and heavy and must've taken it with him." Her eyes filled again with tears. "It puzzled me that Lewis knew Buster was here, but now that I think about it, they must've been in touch while Buster was in jail. I figure they were plan-ning something bad—maybe had even *done* something bad—and Lewis wanted to shut him up."

While Susan went to find Larrimore's address, An-gela questioned the neighbor about Susan Daley. Jill Bickham admitted that it seemed a little odd that Su-san had invited Buster to stay, because she'd hated him like poison. And when Bickham had first seen her standing over the body, Susan had looked disheveled: face flushed, one shoelace untied.

Afterward, alone with the sheriff, Angela said, "She's lying, Chunky."

"Susan Daley?" He blinked. "About what?"

"Buster's friend didn't kill him; Susan did."

Sheriff Jones blinked. "What?"

"That spare room's *too* spare. Too *planned*. Nothing in there but bed, cardtable, chair, and that game."

"Therefore," he said, "no murder weapon."

"Wrong," Angela said. "She had a weapon. I think she took off her sock, filled it with the heavy ball-bear-ings, and bashed him in the head as he slept. She then emptied the balls onto the floor and put her sock back on—but was interrupted by Jill Bickham before she could tie her shoe."

The sheriff pondered that, then frowned. "If that's really what happened . . . how did you know?"

"Because I like board games too," she said, grinning.

MYSTERY:
||||||||||||||||||||||||||||||||||||||||

What tipped Angela off?

39

TROPICAL DEPRESSION

Rᴇᴛɪʀᴇᴅ schoolteacher and amateur crimefighter Angela Potts had been to Florida before—but not as an acting police officer. Sheriff Charles Jones, one of her former students, was attending a regional law enforcement conference in Miami, and she'd talked him into letting her tag along because two representatives had been invited and most of his staff was out sick. The sheriff had reluctantly deputized her and even more reluctantly given her a badge to carry in her purse.

At the moment they were sitting on their hotel's pier, killing time. The day's meetings were over, the humidity was off the charts, and the weather was gloomy. So was the sheriff's mood.

"I must be crazy, bringing you on this trip," he said.

"You are crazy," Angela agreed. "You're also depressed."

"Of course I'm depressed. You should be my wife."

"Thanks, but you're already married."

"You know what I mean. I should've brought her instead."

"She has the flu, Chunky, like half the rest of the town." Angela rose and stretched like a cat. "Besides, she's not a deputy. Let's go eat."

"You're a temporary deputy," he reminded her.

They were about to leave when a young man approached them. "My name's Goodwin," he said, beaming. "Welcome to the tropics."

"This isn't actually the tropics," Angela informed him.

"Sure it is. How about a private boat tour?"

The sheriff scowled. "How much?"

"Fifty bucks."

He and Angela exchanged a look. Why not?

Five minutes later they were seated in Goodwin's small motorboat—his sailboat, he said, was under repair—listening to him spout local color. He told them that Miami has more land area than any other major U.S. city, and that they should avoid the Everglades tours, since it was no more than a stagnant swamp. He also said, pointing ahead and to the right, "There, off the port bow, is where Captain Kidd supposedly hid his treasure." After an hour or so of this, he delivered them back to the pier.

All three climbed out of the boat, and Captain Goodwin gave both his passengers a parting bear-hug. As he turned to leave, though, Angela whispered to the sheriff, "Check your wallet."

He patted his pocket and froze. "It's gone!"

Angela spotted a local cop, but he was too far away to help. Before the sheriff could react she caught up to Goodwin and shoved him, pinwheeling, off the edge of the pier. Then she hailed the policeman.

Moments later they—with the cop's assistance—pulled the dripping Goodwin from the water and pulled the sheriff's wallet, also dripping, from Goodwin's pocket. Sheriff Jones removed the soaked bills and photos and groaned. "Couldn't you maybe have knocked him out instead?"

"Sorry, I'm only a temporary deputy," she reminded him. "Besides, I just had my nails done."

After Goodwin had been handcuffed and escorted away, the sheriff asked her, "How'd you know he picked my pocket?"

"Well, the hug seemed a little strange. And I knew for sure I didn't trust him."

"Why not?"

"Because while you were snoozing on the plane," she said, "I was reading my guidebook."

"What do you mean?"

"I mean Miami doesn't have the most land area of any major city," she said. "It has the *least*. He probably just read that someplace and remembered it wrong. And the Everglades isn't stagnant at all—it's a huge, shallow river, even though it flows at a snail's pace. Everyone knows that."

The sheriff frowned. "I didn't."

"I'm amazed," she said dryly. "And Captain Kidd's treasure is supposed to be buried somewhere on Long Island. That's New York—not here."

"So just about everything he told us was wrong."

She nodded. "Because he made it all up."

The sheriff finished wringing as much water as he could from his wallet, replaced its contents, and squooshed it back into his pocket. "So he isn't a guide."

"He's not even a boat guy," Angela said. "That was the biggest hint that something was amiss. He probably stole it."

"What makes you think that?"

"Because he said something no sailor would say."

MYSTERY:
||||||||||||||||||||||||||||||||||

What had Goodwin said that proved he was an impostor?

40

AS CLEAR AS MUD

"**W**HAT are you doing in town?" the police chief asked, as Sheriff Charles Jones switched off his cell phone. It was nine a.m., in the chief's office at the state capital.

"I attended a seminar yesterday, downtown," Sheriff Jones said. "Heading back home today."

The chief pointed to the sheriff's phone. "Hope that wasn't an emergency call you just got."

"No, that was my former schoolteacher, Angela Potts. She said our jail's empty, as usual."

"She on your staff?"

Sheriff Jones shrugged. "She sometimes thinks she is," he said. "Heck, sometimes *I* think she is."

At that moment, an officer stuck his head into the

room. "We've located Anderson's wife, Chief. She volunteered to drive in—she's waiting in room two."

Chief Randolph excused himself, left the office, and reappeared five minutes later. "We had some excitement yesterday afternoon," he explained to the sheriff. "A local businessman, Larry Anderson, was killed in a downtown parking garage. Blow to the left temple, apparently from behind, as he was about to enter his SUV. It was a rainy day, with cars tracking in mud, and we have footprints from what looks like small-sized sneakers or running shoes. Anyhow, we couldn't reach the wife last night—turns out she was visiting her sister. We only just now got in touch with her. She's upset, of course, but she gave us a good lead: says she was walking in the downtown area yesterday afternoon and at one point saw a guy looking down at her from the roof of the garage where her husband later died."

"Sounds a little too convenient," the sheriff said.

"Who knows. We're still treating it as a lead."

"She only see him that once?"

"Yeah, but says she got a good look. It wasn't raining at the time, and the garage is only three levels."

"Any security cameras?" the sheriff asked.

"Four, at the in- and out-ramps, but none in the garage itself, or the stairwells. Unless the guy she described was driving, we won't see him."

"Described?"

"She said he looked small. Dark shirt, jeans, sneakers, mustache, glasses, blue baseball cap. And—get this—she saw a watch on his right wrist."

They both knew that since the mortal blow was on the left temple and the attack was from behind, the killer was probably left-handed—and they also knew most left-handed men wear their watches on the right arm instead of the left.

"That," the chief said, "plus his size, and the sneakers—well, that all suggests he might be our man."

The sheriff thought that over. "Is the wife still here?"

"Yeah, we need her signature on a couple forms," the chief said. "Personal effects and so on."

"Would you mind if I took them to her?"

"The forms? Why?"

"I'd just like to check something."

The chief shrugged. "Don't see why not. I'll get the papers. But don't say anything to her, okay?"

Ten minutes later Sheriff Jones returned with the signed sheets. "I think you should look closer at Mrs. Anderson," he said to the chief. "Maybe search her house for sneakers, check the soles."

"What?"

"I think she might be your killer."

The chief blinked. "Why would you think that?"

The sheriff pointed to the signatures. "I watched her sign all the forms. She's left-handed."

"So is my minister. I can't arrest someone for being left-handed."

"No—but you can if she lied to you, to throw you off the track." The sheriff leaned forward, both hands propped on the desktop, and carefully revealed his theory to Chief Randolph.

"Good grief," the chief said, wide-eyed. "I think you're right." He snatched up his desk phone, punched a number, and said, "Finley? Don't let Mrs. Anderson leave yet." Then he hung up and said to the sheriff, "How'd you catch it, Jones? Did you learn this kind of thing in your seminar?"

The sheriff smiled. "No," he said. "I learned it from my former schoolteacher."

MYSTERY:
||||||||||||||||||||||||||||||||||||

What told the sheriff Mrs. Anderson was lying, and therefore possibly guilty?

41

DRIVING MISS LACEY

ANGELA Potts sighed as Sheriff Jones leaned forward over the checkerboard and jumped two of her men.

"This makes me feel old," she said. "Look at us—playing checkers in front of the courthouse."

The sheriff, grinning, picked up the jumped pieces. "You *are* old. You taught me in the fifth grade."

"Say that again and I'll stop letting you win."

His grin vanished when he saw Deputy Fred Prewitt waving to them from the sheriff's office across the street. They gathered up their checkers and board, hurried over, and followed Prewitt inside. Standing in front of the sheriff's desk was a young woman with wide, frightened eyes.

"Sheriff, Ms. Potts, this is Charlotte Lacey," Prewitt told them. "Says she was kidnapped."

Tearfully Charlotte gave them her story. Local mechanics Butch and Jed Burkley had shown up at her house half an hour ago, she said, and told her she had to help them rob Hiram Denson's jewelry store, which was closed for the day while Denson was out of town. Charlotte had a key because she sometimes worked there on weekends, and she also knew how to open his safe.

"But I escaped," she said, "before we got there."

"Why'd they take you along?" Angela asked. "Couldn't they have demanded your door key and made you write down the combination?"

"They just told me to come with them." Charlotte's eyes widened even more. "Maybe so they could shoot me, afterward. I sure wouldn't put it past Butch Burkley, or his stupid brother either."

"You know them, then?" the sheriff said.

Her face darkened. "Butch and I was engaged, till last month. He's dating Lucy Mason now."

Sheriff Jones glanced at his deputy. "Better go bring the Burkleys in for questioning, Fred."

"Twenty minutes," Prewitt said, and left.

"Ms. Lacey, do you know if they abducted you in Butch's car, or Jed's?" the sheriff asked.

"Butch's."

"Can you describe it?"

Charlotte shrugged. "It's new and red, is all I know."

"He drives a two thousand twelve Ford coupe," Angela said. "A Focus. It's fire-engine red."

The sheriff raised an eyebrow. "You know cars, Ms. Potts?"

"I know a lot of things."

"How'd you get away from them?" the sheriff asked Charlotte.

"I was sitting between them in the front seat. When Butch stopped at the light on West Main, I socked him in the eye and crawled over into the back seat. I'm pretty quick—I opened his left back door and took off running. Came straight here."

"You did the right thing," the sheriff said.

Fifteen minutes later Prewitt returned with the Burkleys in tow. One of them had a fresh bruise around his right eye. They took a seat, and Sheriff Jones told them Charlotte's story. Both looked surly.

"She's lying, Sheriff," Butch Burkley said. "Lying like a rug. We been working in our garage all day."

"Anybody see you there?"

"Just her." He nodded toward Charlotte. "She didn't know it, but I saw her lurking around outside, this morning."

"What happened to your eye?" Angela asked.

"Jed and me was boxing a little, before breakfast." Butch glared at his brother. "He got me when I weren't looking."

"He's the one who's lying," Charlotte shouted. "I popped him in the eye like I told you, when I escaped."

"Escaped?" Butch said. "From who? Except for a glimpse of you this morning, I ain't even seen your sorry self since I took up with Lucy. That's what she's peeved about, Sheriff. A woman scorned."

"How'd I know about your black eye, then?" Charlotte asked, fuming.

"You probably saw that this morning, spying on us from behind our bushes, and put it into your story. You're as sneaky as ever."

The sheriff sighed and looked at Angela, who rose to her feet and left the room. He followed her.

Outside in the lobby, he said, "What do you think, Ms. Potts? You know these folks better than I do."

"I think you can send 'em all home, Chunky."

"What?"

"I think she made the whole thing up."

"How's that?"

Angela grinned. "Butch was right—jilted women can be dangerous."

MYSTERY:

Why did Angela figure Charlotte Lacey's story was phony?

42

AMOS' LAST WORDS

Retired schoolteacher Angela Potts was driving home from her Saturday morning quilting meeting when she spotted two patrol cars parked beside Denise Fisher's farmhouse. She stopped so fast her tires squealed.

She found Sheriff Charles Jones standing on Fisher's front porch, sour-looking as usual. "Party's over, Ms. Potts," he said. "Case is already closed."

"What do you mean? What's happened?"

"Remember Amos Gautreau? Used to work for Toby Lewis, just down the road?"

"I remember," she said. "Denise told me she hired Amos last week—he works here now."

"Not anymore. He died two hours ago."

"What?!"

The sheriff pointed. "The postman was driving up to the mailbox here when he saw Amos staggering toward him, from the house. Bleeding. According to the postman, Amos said three words: 'Denise shot me.' Then he fell dead."

Angela was stunned. "That's crazy. Denise Fisher wouldn't hurt a fly."

"Amos Gautreau might disagree, if he could. In any case, Denise is in jail. Deputy Wood's inside with the family—he and Ozzie are cousins—and then we're done, here."

The family, Angela knew, consisted of Denise's sister Susan, Susan's husband Ozzie, and their teenaged daughter Rose. Denise, a longtime widow, had hired young Amos Gautreau to help her with all the farmwork that Ozzie was too lazy to do. Sweet, gentle Amos, with his friendly smile and Cajun accent. *How's da world treatin' you?* he would always ask.

Angela shook her head. "Something's wrong."

"Sounds right to me," the sheriff said. "You recall that somebody stole Toby Lewis's stash of cash from his bedroom closet last week? That might explain why Amos left shortly afterward, and hired on with someone else."

"You're saying Amos stole that money?"

"Why not? He had free access to the Lewis house. Maybe he tried to steal from Denise Fisher too."

"What does Denise say?"

The sheriff shrugged. "Says she was out in the toolshed at the time, sharpening a hoe."

"She didn't hear a shot?"

"Not above the noise of the grinder. Another lie, of course, since she's the one who shot him."

"You're wrong," Angela said again.

"Then who did it?"

She thought a moment. "Nobody else heard anything?"

"Denise's sister and Ozzie were at Roscoe's Café—Deputy Prewitt's verified that. The niece, Rose, says she'd walked down to Toby Lewis's place to visit their son Eddie—apparently they've been dating—but nobody was home there."

Angela mulled that over. "Murder weapon?"

"Denise's pistol," the sheriff said. "We found it in her dresser drawer, recently fired and wiped clean of fingerprints."

"So this was planned?"

"Looks like it."

Angela stared into the distance, frowning. "We're forgetting something. I recall Amos reporting that he saw a silhouette of someone sneaking out of Toby Lewis's house the night that cash was stolen—a small woman, with long hair."

"I remember. I figure, now, that he must've been lying, to cover the fact that he stole it himself."

"But if he wasn't, then that description could fit all three women in this house. Denise, Susan, and Rose. And any one of them, not knowing how much Amos had actually seen, might've felt she needed to silence Amos before he revealed her—the thief's—identity."

The sheriff raised an eyebrow. "That's possible. It would establish motive. And since Amos said it was Denise who—"

"But only one of these three women had access to Toby's house," Angela said. "Because she was always there visiting Eddie."

He blinked. "You're saying *Rose* stole the money?"

"I think she did. And I think she shot Amos today, with her aunt's pistol. Rose needed money; rumor has it she's been hinting at getting married and leaving town." Angela paused.

"One more thing: Amos Gautreau was twenty years younger than Denise, and barely knew her. Besides, she was his employer. He wouldn't have used her first name, even to someone else. He'd have said 'Mrs. Fisher.'"

"But the postman heard him, Ms. Potts. Heard Amos say 'Denise shot me.'"

"No," Angela said, smiling. "That's what the postman *thought* he heard."

MYSTERY:

If that was true, then what did Amos
really *say?*

43

DOWN ON THE FARM

Retired schoolteacher Angela Potts was an early riser. Sheriff Charles Jones, one of her less-outstanding former students, was not. He'd even had a tendency to nap during classes, she remembered, and occasionally during town meetings as well.

That's why she was surprised to see a light in his office window at six a.m. on an icy morning.

When she appeared in his doorway he looked up from his desk and growled, "What do you want?"

"A mansion and a million bucks. How about you?"

"I mean why are you here?"

She dropped into a chair. "Bertha Woods is feeling poorly—I spent the night with her. Why are *you* here?"

"Because this is when people do their milking."

"You've taken up dairy farming?"

"No," he said, "but Albert Gooden drives over and milks Herman Mitchell's cow and tends their chickens whenever Hermie and Joyce are out of town." He sighed and rubbed his eyes. "Albert called me a while ago and said the Mitchells' back window's been busted out. He has a house key, and when he went in to look he saw some drawers open and things scattered about."

"He see anyone?"

"Said he'd noticed somebody earlier, walking along the road away from the house. Couldn't tell who it was. When he found the broken window it was too late—the guy was long gone."

Angela perked up. "So let's go out there."

"No need. I called Fred Prewitt, and on his way there he spotted a guy who fit the description. Sure enough, this fella—a drifter named Reardon—admitted he spent the night nearby."

"And?"

"Prewitt's bringing him in."

Both of them heard the cruiser pull up and park outside, and moments later Deputy Prewitt escorted the suspect into the office. Reardon's clothes were filthy, his face lined and weary.

During questioning, he said he'd been hitchhiking cross-country, and the unseasonably frigid weather caused him to seek shelter at what turned out to be the Mitchells' place last night. He found the house locked and nothing but one cow in the rickety barn. But the storm-cellar door was open.

"You took shelter there?" Sheriff Jones asked.

"No sir, not at first. That cellar was big but it was

cold down there, and that drafty barn was worse. But I had to get out of the wind."

"So what'd you do?"

"I led that cow out of the barn and down them cellar steps to the bottom. Got her to lay down, then I curled up beside her to keep warm. Then this morning early, I put her back in her pen."

"You didn't notice a house window broken?"

"It was dark. I tried the front and back doors and that was all."

"Let me get this straight," Angela said. "Faced with freezing to death, you'd rather sleep beside a cow than break into a warm house?"

"It didn't look warm, it just looked empty," Reardon said. "I ain't no vandal, ma'am, nor burglar neither."

Angela studied him a moment, then focused on Prewitt. "Where did you find Mr. Reardon, when you drove out there?"

"He was walking along not far from the Mitchells'."

"Close to the old drive-in movie?"

"Across the road from it."

Angela said, thinking aloud, "It's flat there—he could've seen your car coming a long way off." She looked up. "Did you use your siren?"

"No, but my lights were flashing."

She turned to the sheriff. "You think the helper you told me about—Albert—is still there?"

"Probably. He said he does more chores after the milking."

"Let's call him," she said.

"Albert?"

"Yeah. Let's ask him a favor."

They did just that, and fifteen minutes after that

phone conversation, Albert Gooden reported back. In the weedy ditch across from the drive-in he'd found something, as Angela had suspected he might: a laundry bag containing cash, silverware, and jewelry. When confronted, Reardon confessed that he'd stolen it from the Mitchell house.

While Prewitt showed their new prisoner his cell, the sheriff gave Angela a look. "You knew he was lying, didn't you."

"You should've known, too," she said.

"Why?"

"Because we both grew up on farms."

MYSTERY:

What lie gave Reardon away?

44

AN INSIDE JOB

IT'LL be the perfect crime, James Warren thought.

For one thing, the location was ideal. His idiot boss had built his smalltown law office on cheap land outside the city limits. Besides, luck was on Warren's side: this part of the South rarely saw a winter storm, but tonight it was snowing like a bandit. He had the place all to himself.

Warren parked in the empty lot, pulled on latex gloves, took a boltcutter and a crowbar from underneath his seat, stomped through the falling snow to the building, and used the prybar to splinter the front door. Inside the reception area, he followed his flashlight beam to a door labeled PRIVATE and pried it open as well.

Within seconds he had cut the padlock on the safe in that office and taken out a dozen bundles of cash. Then he used the phone on the desk beside the safe to call the sheriff, identify himself, and report that he was calling from an office that had been burglarized, at his firm's building.

Mission accomplished. He could now—finally—pay off his gambling debts. Smiling, Warren hurried back out to his car, stripped off his gloves, and stowed them in his trunk alongside the tools and packets of cash. Then he trudged back inside to the reception area to wait.

The police arrived within minutes. To his surprise, a gray-haired lady showed up with Sheriff Jones and his deputy. "Who are you?" Warren asked.

"Angela Potts," she said. "Investigative consultant."

That sounded false—she looked more like a bossy grandmother. Before Warren could respond, the sheriff called, from inside the private office, "Did you touch anything in here since you called us?"

"No," Warren said.

"Anything missing except the contents of the safe?"

"Don't know—no one ever uses that office."

While the two lawmen were poking around, the lady—Ms. Potts?—asked, "Why'd you come in on a night like this, Mr. Warren?"

"I often work nights and weekends."

Warren heard Sheriff Jones tell his deputy to fetch his fingerprint kit and check the safe, lock, lights, and everything on the small office's desktop for prints. Several minutes later the sheriff returned to the reception area. "Don't see many padlocks, these days," he said.

Warren shrugged. "My boss isn't too bright." *Why else would he keep a small fortune in cash, on site?* "He's old-fashioned, too."

"Which the burglar must've known," the sheriff said, "since he brought a boltcutter with him."

Warren gulped; he hadn't thought of that.

Thankfully, the sheriff didn't pursue the point. "Did you notice anything outside when you got here, Mr. Warren? Car, truck, van?"

"Nothing," he said. "Not even any tire tracks in the parking lot. Guess the snow covered them."

Ms. Potts said, "I saw *your* tracks were still there, though. Footprints too. Looks like you walked back out of the building to your car's trunk."

Warren blinked. Who *was* this woman? Thinking fast, he said, "I keep work files in my trunk. After I discovered the break-in, I went back out to fetch my phone numbers for the main office, in Jackson—I plan to notify them when you folks are done here."

The deputy stuck his head through the doorway. "We're pretty much done *now*, Sheriff. The only prints I found were on the file cabinets."

"Those would be Millie's—the boss's assistant," Warren said. "She's the only one ever goes in there."

"One more question," Ms. Potts said. She was staring straight at him. "Mind if we check your car trunk?"

Warren's heart skipped a beat. "What?" He glanced at the sheriff and deputy, who appeared to be as confused as he was.

She added, "We can get a warrant, if you like."

"But"—*This can't be happening*, he thought—"Why would you want to search my trunk? Because I left my *footprints in the snow?*"

"It's not what you left that interests me," she said, and smiled. "It's what you didn't leave."

MYSTERY:

What mistake did James Warren make?

45

LICENSE TO STEAL

Rᴇᴛɪʀᴇᴅ schoolteacher Angela Potts had loosened the lug nuts on her back left wheel and was jacking up her car when Sheriff Charles Jones pulled his cruiser into her driveway. "Glad I found you," he said.

She wiped her sweaty forehead. "I didn't know I was lost."

"I need your advice."

"How about a trade? Help me change this flat tire."

He took off his sunglasses and studied the tilted car. "No time. We'll fix it later."

Angela's eyes narrowed. "You're always trying to weasel out of a job."

"No, I'm trying to do *my* job, and solve a robbery. I've

been talking with Ms. Vance—I told her I'd be right back."

"Martha Vance?"

"That's right. Somebody broke into her house. Hop in."

The sheriff briefed her on the way to the crime scene. Ms. Vance had told him she'd heard noises downstairs during an afternoon nap and had looked out a window in time to read the intruder's license plate as he drove away. The sheriff relayed the tag number by phone to the state Department of Motor Vehicles, which immediately traced it to a Wendell Cole, and a local address. Before leaving the Vance home to fetch Angela, the sheriff had made another call, directing Deputy Fred Prewitt to go pick up Mr. Cole.

Angela and the sheriff spent twenty minutes questioning a distraught Martha Vance, who said she was missing a priceless heirloom vase from her dining-room china cabinet. On their drive back downtown Deputy Prewitt phoned them to report that Cole wasn't home, but his landlord had suggested a neighborhood bar Cole often visited after his work at the lumberyard. Prewitt had found him there. A quick search of his car and trunk had revealed nothing incriminating, but Prewitt was now bringing him in for questioning. All four of them met in an interrogation room.

"I'm innocent," Cole said promptly.

The sheriff took a seat. "Your vehicle was seen leaving the home of burglary victim Martha Vance, Mr. Cole. On Lexington Street, around five o'clock."

"Somebody's mistaken. If my car was seen, it was passing by. I take that road home from work."

The sheriff and Angela exchanged worried glances. Lexington was indeed a logical route from the lumberyard to Cole's apartment complex, and to his usual tavern also. Besides that, his car hadn't contained the stolen goods.

"I didn't do it," he said again. "I've never set foot in that woman's dining room, or even in her house. I just happened to use that street to drive home."

The questioning lasted awhile longer, then Prewitt led the suspect to a holding cell. Angela and the sheriff were left alone in the interrogation room.

"Did you know," she said finally, "that Martha's late husband owned the lumberyard here in town?"

The sheriff blinked. "Douglas Vance?"

"If Cole once worked for him—"

"He would've known how rich she is," the sheriff finished. "Why didn't you mention that?"

Instead of answering, she asked him, "How much did you tell Prewitt about the burglary?"

"Prewitt? Nothing. You and I are the only ones who've spoken to Ms. Vance. All Prewitt knew was to bring in the suspect."

"And has Cole talked with anyone else, about this?"

"No. Why?"

For a long moment Angela stared down at her fingers, still greasy from handling the lug nuts on her wheel.

"Let's check his car again," she said.

Ten minutes later the two of them were standing behind Wendell Cole's Honda, in the tavern's parking lot. Angela used his key-remote to open the trunk, peeled back the removable pad that covered the trunk's floor—and smiled. There in the well where the spare tire should have been was an object wrapped in newspaper, and inside the wrapping was Martha Vance's heirloom vase.

The sheriff was stunned. "How'd you know this was here?"

"I didn't," Angela said. "But I figured it had to be around here somewhere."

MYSTERY:
|||||||||||||||||||||||||||||||||||

Why was Angela so certain that Wendell Cole was guilty?

46

HEAR NO EVIL

THE voice on the phone said, "Time to earn your pay."

Sheriff Chunky Jones suddenly felt tired. Calls from his old schoolteacher Angela Potts always had that effect. "What's up, Ms. Potts?"

"A birdnapping," she said. "Lori Dunn just called me—somebody stole her little boy's cockatoo. That's a parrot."

"I know what a cockatoo is."

"I'll meet you at her house."

"Now?" he said. "It's raining. I'll send a deputy."

"You'll go yourself. Remember, it's an election year."

"Parrots can vote, this time?"

"Owners can," she said.

• • •

They arrived to find Lori Dunn and her son Justin sitting in their kitchen. Justin stopped crying long enough to tell them he'd seen someone in a black hooded coat grab Wyatt, one of his two pet cockatoos, out of its cage on the porch and disappear in the rain around the corner of Gertie Morton's house next door. "That's Virgil," Justin said, nodding toward the other parrot's cage.

"Justin likes Westerns," Lori explained.

"They have separate cages?" Angela asked.

"Wyatt's excitable. He tends to throw up."

When asked if she thought Gertie Morton might've seen the thief, Lori said she didn't know, but she supposed it was possible—after all, Wyatt had screamed his head off during the incident.

Angela and the sheriff trooped over to the Morton house and introduced themselves. Gertie seemed friendly enough, but was wearing so much perfume the sheriff almost choked. Her living room was immaculate—oak furniture, grandfather clock, a beige carpet stretching as smooth as unmarked sand between a piano against one wall and a sofa on the other. The sheriff could smell something cooking in the kitchen.

"Any chance," he said, after telling her what had happened, "that you saw anyone run past your house awhile ago?"

"No. I've been playing for hours." She pointed to the piano. A heavy bench was tucked almost out of sight underneath, and a hymn book stood open above the keyboard. "I'm Pentecostal," she added.

"You didn't hear the parrot squawking?" Angela asked her. "They said it was really loud."

"I told you, I was practicing my music. I didn't hear anything, and I didn't see anybody steal Wyatt. Now, if you'll excuse me—"

But she stopped dead, and the sheriff knew why. Angela Potts was watching her with the same slitted eyes that had so terrified him thirty years ago, as a grade-school student.

"Where's the parrot, Ms. Morton?" Angela asked.

"What?"

"The sheriff can get a search warrant. Do we need one?"

Gertie Morton's shoulders sagged. "No," she groaned. "The bird's at my sister's, down the street."

"Why'd you take him?" Angela asked.

Gertie slumped even further. "He screamed all the time, day and night, that parrot. Dern thing ran me crazy. My sister and I were going to give him to our cousin, over in Greenwood. She'd give him a good home." Then she looked up. "How'd you know? Because I called him Wyatt?"

"That helped," Angela said. "If you saw nothing and haven't yet talked with the Dunns, how could you know which of the two parrots was stolen? But there was also the perfume, and the piano."

"Perfume?"

"My Pentecostal friends," Angela said, "don't usually wear perfume or cologne."

Gertie nodded. "I should've known, I guess—I'd heard them say Wyatt throws up occasionally." She sniffed her sleeve. "You should see my coat."

"And you figured the perfume would cover the smell."

Another nod. "It belongs to my niece. I splashed some on when I saw you and the sheriff headed over here."

She wiped her eyes. "Am I under arrest?"

"You're under orders to return the parrot, and apologize to the Dunns. That okay with you, Chunky?"

Sheriff Jones, who was gaping at them both, blinked. "Sure."

As they turned to leave, Gertie said, "What about the piano?"

"Excuse me?" Angela said.

"You said there were two more things. The perfume and the piano."

"Yes." Angela gave her a sad smile. "Too bad you don't play more often."

MYSTERY:
||||||||||||||||||||||||||||||||||||||

Why did Angela figure Gertie Morton was
the birdnapper?

47

CHECKMATE

Sнeriff Charles Jones and Deputy Fred Prewitt were strolling to Roscoe's café for breakfast when they saw a wide-eyed woman in a maid's uniform rush out the front door of Judge Leonard Moore's house. "Come quick," she called to them. "He's dead."

The Judge was indeed dead, of a gunshot wound to the chest; his body was slumped in a desk chair in his study. The maid said she'd found him only moments ago, when she'd arrived for the day. On the desktop in front of him was a chessboard on a swivel base—the kind that allows one person to play both sides. The chesspieces had all been removed except one: a white knight, standing alone in the middle of the board.

After checking the rest of the house, the sheriff said, "No signs of forced entry. The killer must've been invited in, or had a house key."

"Either way, the Judge saw him," Prewitt said. "The desk faces the room."

The sheriff pointed to the lone chesspiece. All the others were scattered across the desktop. "Know what Ms. Potts would say about this, Fred?" Angela Potts, the sheriff's former schoolteacher, loved mysteries the way the sheriff loved peach cobbler.

"She'd probably say she wished she were here," Prewitt said, "instead of home with bronchitis."

"No, she'd say there's a chance that the victim left us a dying message."

"A message? You mean, like a clue?" Prewitt asked. "If so, why not write it? Surely there's a pen and paper in the desk."

"Maybe there wasn't time." The sheriff looked again at the only piece on the board: a rearing white stallion. "I don't play chess much—what's that one called? A horse?"

"A knight."

"Hmm." After a moment he turned to the sniffling maid. "Ms. Wilson, who else has a key to the house?"

"Only three people. The Judge's children—Matthew, Clayton, and Ruth." She shook her head sadly. "They don't come to visit often, though."

"Well, I need 'em to come now," the sheriff said. "Fred, fetch all three—the sons own Moore Hardware and the daughter works at the courthouse. Just quietly tell them the Judge was found dead. No other details."

Ten minutes later Judge Moore's three offspring were ushered into the living room. All of them looked shocked. Clayton was the first to speak, muttering, "This is terrible."

Matthew gave him a withering look. "Especially for you, Clay—who'll you ask for money now?"

Their sister Ruth sighed. "For once, can the two of you get along?"

"He was a good father," Matthew said solemnly.

"Who could've killed him, Sheriff?" Clayton asked.

"Can we see the body?" Ruth said.

"When do you think it happened?" Matthew asked.

Sheriff Jones stopped them with a raised hand. "First things first," he said. "Clayton—you are under arrest for the murder of your father. Fred, read him his rights."

The sister gasped. "What!? Clay, what have you done?"

Clayton's face, which had lost all its color, reddened again. "What have *I* done?" He pointed a trembling finger at Ruth. "It was all *her* idea, Sheriff. She wanted his inheritance as bad as I did."

In the stunned silence that followed, the sheriff managed to hide his surprise; he hadn't suspected an accomplice. "No problem," he said. "We have more than one cell."

Twenty minutes later, Sheriff Jones and Prewitt were sitting together in the sheriff's office. An astonished Matthew Moore had been sent home and both his siblings were in custody.

"How in the world did you know?" Prewitt asked.

"About Clayton? Two things," the sheriff said. "First, the chess set. The only piece left on the board was a white horse."

"So?"

"As it turned out, the Judge *did* leave us a message.

Remember Silver, from *The Lone Ranger*? On TV?"

"Sure."

"The Lone Ranger's real name was Clayton Moore."

Prewitt blinked. "Seriously?"

"I love Westerns," the sheriff admitted.

"But still—that's not enough to make an arrest. You said *two* things."

MYSTERY:

What convinced the sheriff that Clayton was guilty?

48

ANDY, GET YOUR GUN

ANDY Garner was kneeling behind the counter of his roadside café, packing, when retired teacher Angela Potts came in.

"Mornin', Angel," he said. "Guess you're here to say goodbye."

"Unless I can talk you into staying."

She plopped down on a stool across from him. Outside the back window, it was a clear, calm day; somebody was burning leaves in the distance, the smoke rising straight up into a wide blue sky.

Garner smiled. "Not me. I'm heading up north. Bought a house near my grandkids." Andy Garner had recently done the seemingly impossible: he drove across the river to the next state to buy a lottery ticket—and won. Now, half a million dollars richer, he was finally retiring. Angela couldn't have been happier for him.

"Got that first payment yet?" Angela asked.

"Two days ago—never saw that much money in one place in my life."

"Hang onto it," she said. "You're a popular man now, Andy, and not just to your friends."

"I'll be careful," he assured her. "But I sorta doubt my newfound fortune is national news—"

He stopped in mid-sentence as two men in overalls pushed through the front door. Angela turned and watched them take seats beside her at the counter.

"Sorry, gents," Garner said. "We're closed. But there's a Burger King just down the road a ways."

Both men studied him in silence, gave Angela a long look, and then turned back to Garner. "That's a shame," one of them said. "Sign said 'diner.' Now you're saying we can't dine?"

"The signs have been taken down," Angela said to them. "How'd you know to stop here?"

The first man hesitated, but the second one pointed to a color picture on the wall behind Garner. "Your flag's still up, outside." The photo showed a blue flag flying above the building, a flag with the words ANDY'S DINER in big block letters.

"Even so," Garner said, "I'm no longer open. Wish I could help you."

The two men stared back at him, saying nothing. As the tension mounted, Angela pulled out a notepad, scrawled on it, tore off a sheet, and handed it to Garner.

"Here's my address," she said. "Keep in touch, okay?"

She slid off the stool and walked out the front door.

She forced herself not to look back. The note she'd written had said GET YOUR GUN. I'M CALLING THE SHERIFF. She knew Garner kept a loaded revolver behind the counter, and she also knew the sheriff's office was only a block away. Angela took out her phone and hit speed dial on the way out the door, then stopped to look at the license number on the two men's old Mercury before climbing into her own car.

Sheriff Jones and his deputy responded fast—they were already pulling into the diner's lot by the time she'd driven a quarter mile down the street. She U-turned, roared back to the café, parked beside the patrol car, and hurried inside.

The situation was well in hand. Andy Garner was pointing his pistol at the two strangers while the sheriff and deputy applied handcuffs and relieved them of their weapons. Both men were wanted, the sheriff told her, for two robberies upstate. The sheriff hadn't yet had time to run the license plates Angela had given him, but the Mercury fit the description of the getaway car. One of the men even had a newspaper clipping in his pocket about Andy's lottery win.

When the prisoners had been taken away, Angela sat again on the stool across from Andy Garner. He looked shaken but okay. He tucked his gun back into the alcove below the counter. "Thanks, Angel," he said. "And I suppose you were right—word's already out about my jackpot."

"The price of celebrity," Angela said, smiling.

"How did you know?" he asked. "For sure, I mean? How'd you know they didn't really just see my flag and stop for a bite to eat?"

"Because I'm observant," she said. "Want some help with the packing?"

MYSTERY:

*How **did** Angela know they were lying?*

49

GOING FOR THE GOLD

WHEN Angela Potts barged into the sheriff's office she found him leaned back in his chair with his boots on the desktop—but that wasn't unusual. Also on his desktop was the combo TV/VCR from the outer office, and he was staring at it so hard he didn't even hear her come in. That *was* unusual.

"I haven't seen you that focused," she said, "since the tri-county beauty contest. You watching a Western or a ballgame?"

"I'm tired of Westerns," Sheriff Jones said, without looking up.

"What's the score, then?"

He glanced at her, then went back to the TV.

"Criminals one, businessmen zero."

"What?"

He punched a button on his remote and swiveled the screen so she could see it. The grainy picture showed a countertop, a lobby, and a glass door.

"Dalton's Gold Exchange, on Mulberry," he said. "I just got back—I've been there all afternoon."

He pressed PLAY, and Angela saw the top of a man's bald head move into the frame and then duck down suddenly, out of the picture. She also heard the POP of a gunshot. Then the screen went blank.

"What happened?" she asked.

"According to witnesses, someone shot the camera. Fortunately, the tape was in a separate unit."

"What witnesses?"

"The storeowner—Wade Dalton—and two employees, Eddie Ruiz and Arthur Lane. They say a masked gunman came in through a locked alley door around noon today, shot the security camera, and took two pounds of gold coins and ingots. They're—"

"I know what ingots are," Angela said.

"Well, he stole 'em, and got away clean."

"Why don't I recognize these names?"

"It's a new store," he said. "They buy, sell, and trade anything gold. Watches, rings, teeth, you name it." He pointed to the TV. "The owner's the only one on this part of the tape—the others are behind the counter."

"Descriptions?"

The sheriff shrugged. "Dalton's a big guy, baldheaded, golf shirt, penny loafers, khakis; Ruiz is young, dark, T-shirt, jeans; Lane's young too, blond crewcut, coveralls, sneakers, tattoos. During questioning, all three were cooperative . . . but really nervous."

Angela pondered that for a moment. "You're thinking it was an inside job?"

"I'm thinking there was inside knowledge. Otherwise gold ingots would be hard to sell, without attracting attention. And the suspect probably came through the back because he knew exactly where the only camera was. I'd bet one of these three was in on it."

"I agree. Maybe the same one who unlocked the back door so the guy could get in."

"The unlocker could've been Wade Dalton." The sheriff reran the tape to show the moment when the top of Dalton's head entered the frame. "He walks in from that direction."

"Why does he disappear from the picture, all of a sudden?"

"I wondered that myself. He's facing away from where the gunman would be, and at first I thought he just ducked, at the sound of the shot. But—"

"But he ducks *before* the shot's fired," Angela said. "Right? Otherwise we wouldn't see him do it."

"Correct. Which means maybe he already knew someone was behind him, and was *about* to shoot the camera. Which would implicate him." The sheriff hit the STOP button. "We viewed the tape on site, and I asked Dalton about that. He said he wasn't ducking—he was bending down to tie his shoe. Says he didn't see the robber behind him until he heard the shot. That would explain what we see on the tape."

"What about the two employees?" Angela asked.

"Suspicious. Ruiz has a misdemeanor record long as my arm, and Lane served time for insurance fraud."

"Which is what *this* could be."

"But nothing's solid. What's frustrating is that if one

of them *is* the inside accomplice, and if I could find and charge him, I could squeeze him to name the robber." The sheriff shook his head. "But I don't know which one's guilty."

Angela grinned from ear to ear. "I do. It's Wade Dalton."

MYSTERY:

How did Angela figure it out?

50

HILDY'S FORTUNE

ANGELA Potts was eating breakfast at home when her phone rang. It was Ruby Ann Griffin at the bank, asking if Angela knew why their mutual friend Hildy Price hadn't come in to work yet. "She's never been late before," Ruby Ann said. "I'm worried."

Angela knew what had probably happened. An article in last week's newspaper, intended to be a tribute to the recent death of Hildy's estranged multi-millionaire father, had caused Hildy some problems. An only child, never married, Hildy lived alone and had led a quiet and happily uneventful life—until the appearance of the article. Since then, she'd received dozens of requests for donations, loans, even outright gifts. She was probably lying low for a while, Angela figured. It *was* surprising, though, that she hadn't called to inform her boss of her absence.

"I'll check on her," Angela promised.

Hildy still lived in the farmhouse that her father had abandoned—he'd also abandoned Hildy and her mother—to seek greener pastures. Angela parked in the gravel driveway behind two other cars: Hildy's and a unfamiliar black Nissan with Alabama plates. A man with an equally unfamiliar face answered Angela's knock at the front door. "Might I help you?" he asked.

"You might," Angela said. "I'm looking for Hildy Price."

"I'm afraid she's not feeling well. I'm her nephew, visiting from Mobile. Could you come back another time?"

For a moment Angela studied him in silence. Polite, casually dressed, probably late twenties.

Finally she said, "Actually, I came to ask her about a lantern she borrowed from me, for her storm cellar. Turns out I'll need it today."

"The storm cellar?"

"Right." Angela stepped back from the door and pointed. "She never keeps it locked. Mind if I pop in there and fetch my lantern?"

"Be my guest," he said. "Need any help?"

"Actually, there *are* some tall steps just inside. Would you be kind enough to get it for me?"

"Sure. Show me the way."

Angela led him to a large wooden trapdoor set in the grass of the side yard. Sure enough, the door was closed but unlocked; she bent and unhooked the open padlock from its latch, then the young man pulled the door open with a squeak of hinges. Rough stairs led down into darkness.

"Step careful," she said, pointing. "Hildy told me she keeps the lantern just ahead, there."

As soon as the young man had disappeared into the cellar, Angela let the door drop shut. Swiftly she slapped the padlock through the latch and closed the lock with a CLICK. A muffled shout came from below, followed by pounding and curses.

Angela paid no attention. She hurried back to the house and within minutes found Hildy Price bound to a chair in the kitchen. The drawers were all out and over-turned, and the other rooms were in similar disarray.

"Thank goodness," Hildy gasped, when Angela removed her gag. "Whoever that is—he's been turning the house upside down. Every so often he's been coming back and asking me where my money's hidden." She paused, her face stark white. "Where IS he?"

"Locked in the storm cellar," Angela said. "He'll soon be locked up downtown." She untied Hildy's ropes, then phoned the sheriff on her cell and told him to come quick.

"Who is he?" Hildy asked.

"Probably just somebody who reads the newspapers."

"I could hear you talking to him on the porch." She was beginning to regain some of her color. "What made you think something was wrong?"

"Something he said. By the way, *do* you have a fortune hidden?"

Hildy chuckled without humor. "Not a dime. All Daddy's wealth is willed to his second wife."

"How about a key to the storm cellar? You have one of those?

"A key to that big padlock? Oh my, no. I don't know where that could be."

Angela couldn't help smiling. "What a shame," she said.

MYSTERY:

Why had Angela suspected that the young man was up to no good?

SOLUTIONS

||||||||||||||||||||||||||||||||||||||||||||||||||||

1 Wild Goose Chase

Why was Angela so sure they would catch the escapee?

Because she knew he'd have to stop someplace soon and switch cars. If the Jeep was stolen *while in line, waiting for a gas pump*, it had to be low on fuel.

2 Caught on Tape

What proof was Angela referring to?

The image they were watching on the tape was a reflection in a mirror behind the cash registers. Billy Moore was actually eating and drinking with his *right* hand—not his left.

3 It's About Time

Why did Angela suspect Bernie Walton?

Blood from a wound last night at ten would have dried by the time he knelt beside her body this morning at eight. The bloodstain on his coat must have happened last night instead.

4 Gone Goes the Weasel

Who was the thief?

Leah Jean Cimaron. Her name, when "whittled down" to remove the Jean and "turned around"—spelled backward—is Nora Michael.

5 Stick 'Em Up

Why did Angela suspect that Judy was the accomplice?

If the robber came in wearing sunglasses and kept both hands on the briefcases the whole time, he couldn't have removed the glasses—so Judy couldn't have *seen* the color of his eyes.

6 High Finance

Why did Angela figure "Reynolds Whitworth" was the guilty party?

If it was almost five o'clock in L.A., it was almost eight on the East Coast. Any broker would know that the New York Stock Exchange had closed hours ago.

7 A Shot in the Dark

Why did Angela already suspect that George Glenn was the killer?

Because he had asked, *before he'd been told how his aunt had died,* "You think *I* shot her?"

8 Purple Martin

What gave Martin Russell away?

If he really lived out of state, he wouldn't have been so familiar with a local weathercaster.

9 Par for the Course

What made Angela think Rollie Jones was guilty?

An electric golf cart is silent; Wilma wouldn't have heard Parnell pull into the driveway. Since Rollie was the only other person with a house key, the car motor she heard must have been his.

10 A Room for Three

Which person had the face that Angela could match with a name?

Reverend Barnes. From their conversation—if there were only three people—the clergyman had to be the woman.

11 Liar, Liar

What convinced Angela that Laura Hinson was the one who was lying?

Since their meeting was Sunday, and the accident happened "the day before yesterday," and since it had rained all day Friday—there couldn't have been a dust cloud to obscure Laura's vision.

12 The President's Residence

What made Angela think that somebody was currently living in the house?

The ticking of the old clock. Since it was running, someone had been here to wind it.

13 A Quick Stop

Which of Crawford's lies first made Angela suspicious?

If he was traveling east (Texas to Georgia), the late afternoon sun couldn't have been in his eyes.

14 In Other Words

*How **did** Angela know which niece was guilty?*

Because the senator had the correct letters to spell out "Edith," if he'd needed to. What he *didn't* have were the letters necessary to spell either of Mary's names, first or last.

15 Highway Robbery

Why did Angela think the thief was Russell Brown's former partner?

Because Brown was from Sydney. The word "mate," spoken with an Aus-*trigh*-lian accent, would sound like what she'd thought she heard him say: "might."

16 A Dirty Trick

How did Angela know Betty Clarkson was lying?

The tape showed the robber wearing gloves. Clarkson couldn't have seen the back of his hand.

17 The Rules of the Game

Why did Angela think Kevin Bassett was innocent?

Because Brittany couldn't have seen Kevin in a dark jersey when he left the field that day. In high school baseball, the home team typically wears white—only the visiting team wears colored uniforms.

18 A Cold Case

What made Angela suspect that the realtor wasn't on the level?

He was lying about the drive. There are no roads to or from Juneau, Alaska; it can be reached only by plane or boat.

19 Angela's Taxi

What convinced Angela that Jeffrey Boone was the murderer?

Boone said, before the sheriff had mentioned anything about the time of Arnold's death, "I was right here at home last night."

20 A Warm Welcome

What made Angela think Frank Morrison was in the house?

When she sat down, the seat of her chair was still warm. And what other secret visitor would Cordelia have had?

21 This Seat's Taken

Why was Angela convinced the escapees hadn't carjacked Susan's Civic?

There wouldn't have been room for them, or time for them to make room. Her vehicle contained two children's carseats.

22 The Cover-Up

What tipped Angela off?

If Jenny's "kidnappers" had handkerchiefs over their lower faces, she wouldn't have been able to see a mustache.

23 Ollie's Folly

How did Angela know that Ollie Mayfield had been in the house?

If he hadn't, he wouldn't have known which closed door led to the kitchen.

24 The Truth Stings

Why did Angela suspect that Marge had mis-identified the killer?

If a flashlight's beam was shining at you on an otherwise black night, there's no way you could see who's holding it.

25 Turn Right at the Light

How did Angela first know something was amiss?

House number 318 couldn't be *across the street* from 316. If it was an even number it would be next door.

26 Better Late Than Never

Why did Angela suspect that the woman was in on the robbery?

No female customer—especially an out-of-towner—would be standing in a teller line, waiting to do a transaction, without either a purse or pockets.

27 Puppy Love

How did Angela know Lisa Ford was lying?

Dalmatian puppies don't have spots until they're a couple of weeks old. If Ford had really seen them she'd have realized that.

28 Watch Your Step

What was the clue that told him Gumbo Harris had been murdered?

If nobody'd been up there since the incident, and the door was closed, whoever pushed him must have closed it. If he'd fallen out on his own, on a windless day, the door would still be open.

29 Homeland Security

What had convinced Angela that the man was guilty?

He wasn't a guest of the hotel—or at least not of *that* hotel. Their room locks were activated by cards, not keys.

30 No Trespassing

Which of the three young men was lying?

Jim Santos. He said his mother, supposedly in Argentina, was having a hard winter—but when it's winter in the U.S. it's *summer* in the Southern Hemisphere.

31 The Family Jewels

What made Sheriff Jones suspect that Danny Fowler was lying?

Suspenders and belts are designed to hold up trousers. Nobody wears both at the same time.

32 Heat Wave

What made Angela doubt the woman's story?

Janice Burke couldn't have been walking barefoot, on the blistering-hot asphalt—and neither could the imaginary thief.

33 Number, Please

What had Angela noticed that pointed her toward Zack and Ned French?

FXH-EIST, on a telephone keypad, is 394-3478. That's the Frenches' phone number.

34 The Listener

What did Angela hear that convinced her Jack Nelson was guilty?

He said Prewitt took him "back" to Sullivan's house. If he'd never been there before, how could he go *back*?

35 Bus Stop

Why was Angela certain that Norm Kimbrough's heroic story was false?

Kimbrough couldn't have opened the front door of the schoolbus from the outside. The driver had to have opened it, with the hand lever, and he couldn't have done that if already unconscious.

36 Picture This

Why had Angela suspected that the man they'd seen had robbed the bank?

Because if Thursday was three days ago, today was Sunday. And banks aren't open on Sunday.

37 Breaking News

What made Angela think Trudy Martin was lying?

Baby monitors pick up sounds in addition to those that children make. If someone had broken the baby's window to get in, Trudy—a light sleeper anyway—should have heard it.

38 Game Plan

What tipped Angela off?

You can't play Chinese checkers if all the marbles look the same—as was the case with the ball bearings. Nobody'd know whose pieces were whose.

39 Tropical Depression

What had Goodwin said that proved he was an impostor?

The right side of a boat is *starboard*. Not port.

40 As Clear as Mud

What told the sheriff Mrs. Anderson was lying, and therefore possibly guilty?

If she only got one look, from street level, at the "mystery man" on the roof of the garage, she couldn't have seen what kind of shoes he was wearing.

41 Driving Miss Lacey

Why did Angela figure Charlotte Lacey's story was phony?

Ford Focus coupes—and most other coupes, as opposed to sedans—are two-door, not four-door. Charlotte couldn't have crawled into the back seat and opened a rear door to get out, the way she said she had.

42 Amos' Last Words

*If that was true, then what did Amos **really** say?*

Amos probably didn't say "Denise"—he said "da niece."

43 Down on the Farm

What lie gave Reardon away?

You can't lead a cow *down* a stairway; only *up.*

44 An Inside Job

What mistake did James Warren make?

He'd left his latex gloves on when he used the office phone to call the sheriff. His fingerprints should've been on the receiver.

45 License to Steal

Why was Angela so certain that Wendell Cole was guilty?

Because of what he said during questioning. If he were innocent, and hadn't been told any details of the crime, he couldn't have known the stolen item had been "in the dining room."

46 Hear No Evil

Why did Angela figure Gertie Morton was the birdnapper?

Since the piano bench was tucked away underneath and no marks were visible on the floor behind it, Gertie had to be lying. If someone had been playing recently, the bench's legs would've made impressions on the smooth carpet.

47 Checkmate

What convinced the sheriff that Clayton was guilty?

Clayton asked, "Who could've killed him?" At that point he'd been told only that his father *was found dead*—not that he'd been murdered.

48 Andy, Get Your Gun

*How **did** Angela know they were lying?*

Because they couldn't have read the words on the flag outside the cafe. On a windless day, with leaf smoke rising straight up into the sky, the flag would've been hanging down and unopened.

49 Going for the Gold

How did Angela figure it out?

Because Dalton lied when he said he bent over to tie his shoe. Penny loafers are slip-ons; they don't have laces.

50 Hildy's Fortune

Why had Angela suspected that the young man was up to no good?

Because he couldn't be who he said he was. An only child who's never been married can't *have* a nephew.